EVERYONE IS AWFUL

Everyone Is Awful

A Short Story Collection

George T Riley

For Peter, my writing and comedy mentor.

CONTENTS

THE KING IS DEAD, PART I

10th June 2017. Las Vegas, Nevada.

Summer in Vegas was blistering. Sidewalks cracked, tarmac buckled and the city smog shimmered like a mirage. Few could handle the heat outside for more than a half hour before crawling into the nearest air-conditioned sanctuary. Carlos was one of those few.

His days were devoted to walking those streets, no matter how punishing the heat. Carlos saw it all. The homeless who saved up for a bag of ice to sling over their shoulders, so they could appeal to cocktail-slurping tourists on the strip, before retreating to the sewage drains for shelter, the only place cool enough for respite. He saw visitors diving into the Bellagio fountains, only to be promptly wrestled out by security and dispatched from sight. He'd even seen people collapsed from exhaustion, having wandered too far beyond the famous sign, the desert's toll on this oasis.

But hardship was in Carlos's blood, and so was resistance. His skin had long since wrinkled and darkened, his eyes clouded despite the diamond blue shades he wore.

1

For a man in his fifties, he was limber; muscles lean and soles firm from long days on his feet. He'd survived a childhood in the slums of Mexico, made it across the border – legally – fought racism and bigotry to carve out a life and career for himself. True, fortunes had diminished in the years since the King's demise, but Carlos had *survived*. Through it all, he had lasted. Until today.

•

The morning ritual began at 5AM. Carlos rose, stretched, ate a slice of peanut butter on toast, and started his transformation. The one luxury in his basic room was the dressing table, which he'd discovered in an antique store many years ago, just as he was getting started in the city. It had brought him much luck in that time. A Hollywood star's dresser, it featured a large mirror edged with globe-shaped bulbs, which Carlos lit up every day.

He checked his hair. Shoulder length, bleach blonde, no roots showing. The King would never have roots. Carlos combed it through, fixing it with spray into a luxurious bouffant.

The face was simple. A dab of concealer, massage of moisturiser into the leathery folds of skin, some colour to the lips.

Carlos chose the day's outfit from the freestanding rack of costumes he'd accumulated. Each element was a signature part of the look, all crucial in their form, even if he mixed up the design. Smart white shirt with a grandad collar. Rich red, diamanté studded braces. Sequined black jacket with flared sleeves and a white diamond pattern on the back. Sharp rouge trousers, also flared. Glossy black shoes, with a solid heel to tap a beat as he strolled down the strip. The final touch was the sunglasses, composed of diamond-shaped blue lenses.

Carlos looked in the mirror. Dante DaSilva, the late King of Cool, smouldered back at him.

By 6.30, Carlos was making his way to the strip. His studio apartment was about a forty-five minute walk from the heart of Sin City, so he'd arrive in time for the early bird breakfasters. The streets were relatively quiet, but they would soon clog like the arteries of Vegas's visitors, revellers and gamblers from across the globe seeking complete escape from the real world. Carlos loved it.

As he passed glass-fronted eateries, filling up with customers starting their day on a heap of syruped pancakes and frozen margaritas, he caught a few staring at him. Even though they wouldn't be able to tip him from the restaurant, he treated them to a few of the King's classic dance moves, tapping his feet in and out, thrusting his hips and jabbing his fingers in the air. There was always the chance they'd pass him on the street later and sling him a few notes.

But strangely none of the diners were responding with the usual smiles, waves or claps. Some gawped, others hastily turned their gaze back to their gloopy piles of carbs. Carlos shrugged and strolled on. Some days were tougher than others.

Carlos adored his job. Being an impersonator was never something you could dream of as a child, or even plan for – as how could you imagine who you might grow up to look like? He didn't really see his job as impersonation anyway. Once Carlos put on those glasses, he *became* Dante DaSilva, the platinum-selling, international pop icon. As he was growing up, he watched Dante bloom from singer to sensation. Witnessing a brown-skinned Latino breaking through onto the global stage in the eighties blew his mind.

3

To see someone who looked like him – in fact, a *lot* like him – making it so big was an inspiration. It gave him the confidence to pursue his own musical talents, get a US visa and – after limited success under his own name – shift into the impersonation business. Dressing up in Dante's trademark style and auditioning hard got him a few gigs in clubs across the south before, at the peak of the King's success, he landed a regular slot at the casinos in Vegas. Those were the good years. He adored seeing the joy in the faces of his audience as he belted out Dante's hits. But like many things, feelgood pop was of its era. The King of Cool had earned an eternal position in history, but brighter stars were burning. And in 2007, he died aged forty-nine.

Carlos was now older than his icon would ever be, but he kept the great man's spirit alive, even if he no longer got the casino bookings, even if he had to make his living through pacing the strip all day every day, dressed in character, posing for photographs, dancing, singing, surviving on tips. The lifestyle was tough, but he lived for the reward of the joy of fans seeing their hero once more.

A man spat at him as he passed. 'Fucking jerk,' he muttered. Carlos was too stunned to react. By the time he turned to look, the obese gent had waddled into a sports bar. He used the toe of one shoe to try to wipe the saliva from the other. Carlos had to assume the man was drunk, which wasn't unusual for a morning in Vegas.

A steady flow of people moved between coffee shops, restaurants and casinos as the sun started to cook the city. Carlos paused for a break on a bench round the side of the Flamingo, eating the sandwich he'd packed. The price of food on the strip was exorbitant, so he always made sure to come prepared. He'd often bring a little extra, like a pack of salted nuts or beef jerky, that he could share with the rough sleepers – Carlos knew what it was like to be in need.

When he returned to the throng, the staring of passers-by intensified. People skirted out of his way, expressed shock or even disgust when he tried to engage with them. A few such reactions he could dismiss; there were always some who were indifferent or dismissive of street performers. But this was something else.

He crossed over the gargantuan road towards the Bellagio, where the regular fountain display was in full swing. He could usually attract a decent audience from the crowds that gathered there.

The final cascades of water were collapsing as he made it across the many lanes of traffic and there was a smattering of applause as people began to disperse. Carlos spotted a couple with their little girl staying behind in the shade of a leafy tree. Kids loved Dante DaSilva, both the charismatic entertainer when he was alive and the performers who donned his extravagant costumes in his absence.

Carlos approached the family, trotting a rat-tat-tat on his heels. The little girl took notice, curious, one hand linked in her mother's. Carlos spun round on his toes, crouched down and gave her a wave.

'Hi there, my sweetie!' he called. 'Would you like a photo with the King of Cool?'

He could tell the child was reticent, but interested. Then the mother shrieked.

'Oh God!' she cried. 'Terry!'

Terry, the father, spun to look at what had provoked such fear in his partner. 'What the stinking hell?' He heaved himself between Carlos and his family, a fleshy barrier, digital camera swinging from a strap round his neck. 'Get out of here, you creep!'

Carlos was astonished. He couldn't understand what he'd done to ignite such fury.

'Terry, get him away!' the mother said, cradling her daughter in a tight bind. The girl began to whimper.

'You're a bloody sick man,' Terry growled at Carlos. 'Shame on you, you perverted creep. Get the hell away from my family, before I call the cops.'

Onlookers were beginning to gather, *flies to shit*, as Carlos's mother used to say, and Carlos felt like the shit. Lips curled, whispers, jeers, phones flashing, filming. Carlos stumbled back to his feet. 'I'm sorry,' was all he could mutter.

'Check the news, freak!' someone shouted at his back, as he jogged away down the street.

His breath ragged, a thousand glares in the crowd became a blur as he staggered through it. The midday heat was searing, too relentless for him to run. He made it to the edge of the strip, seeking escape in an air-conned 7-Eleven. The cashier, a teen on his phone, barely spared Carlos a glance.

Carlos got his breath back by the fridges, resting his forehead on the cool glass. Then he turned to the racks of newspapers. One story dominated, screaming across the papers. He picked up *The New York Times*. It took an age for the words of the headline to sink in.

THE KING OF CRUEL: DANTE DASILVA'S DECADES OF HORRIFIC CHILD ABUSE EXPOSED.

Blood throbbed in his neck, his temple, as he rushed through the article. A revelatory documentary aired on NBC the night before. Three-year investigation. All those rumours, long dismissed as sick hearsay by devoted fans, proven true. Young men and women putting their stories on record. Photographic evidence unearthed. Lurid details. Corroboration. Undeniable. Despicable. A legacy destroyed. A monster.

Strength flooded out of him, leaving him cold in the head. So this is why they detested him. The icon of joy and positivity that he represented had become a demon, a malicious, manipulative monster. How could DaSilva have done such evil things? There had been gossip, even before his death, but Carlos, and the public at large, had always taken them to be unfounded cynicisms. People unable to accept that a man could become so successful and remain kind and innocent, while sharing such affection with his young fans. Sure, the parties at the Castle had seemed a little unusual, but only out of the context of his flamboyant persona. And his only adult relationship had collapsed soon after the birth of his child, but weren't all celebrity romances doomed?

'You gonna buy that, bud?' the cashier asked.

'Sorry,' Carlos said, returning the paper and walking from the store in a daze. 'Actually…' He stopped, pointing to a shelf behind the counter. 'I'll take one of those.'

•

Carlos walked. It was all he could do. Past giant casinos and malls, he walked, but he could not outpace the black cloud that had descended so rapidly upon him. This was his life, his everything, sullied to the core. He was powerless to pay for another man's crimes, a man that he had loved and admired for decades. The man that had inspired him to rise above his meagre origins and make something of himself, despite all the rejection and

7

persecution. All his success had been built on DaSilva; he'd made nothing on his own. And now what was left for an old man?

Cold liquor down his throat, his mouth already numb. Hand scrunched around the bottle's brown paper covering. He barely drank these days, having made such an effort to cut down after it had cost him his marriage at the height of his casino fame. But when he did drink, he drank hard.

The sun set, giving the city's residents some mercy from its blaze. Red eyed, bottle in hand, Carlos was relieving himself against a wall on the outskirts of the gambling sprawl. He was still dressed in the King's clothes, so intrinsic were they to him, he barely owned anything else. Why go home? Why change? What would there be to wake to tomorrow?

'Oh my god,' came a voice to his left. Sniggering. Whispers. 'What the fuck?'

Carlos swayed towards the sounds, his vision taking a moment to catch up. He focused on the approaching figures. Two men, two women, coming in the direction of the Stratosphere, from the look of it nearly as inebriated as himself.

'Eurgh!' one of the ladies squealed, pointing at his crotch before he had a chance to make himself decent.

'Filthy perv,' the other said.

Carlos started to back away, turning on his heels.

'He's done up as that paedo,' one of the men said. 'What the fuck, dude?'

Carlos walked away, feet slapping on the sidewalk. But the group followed him.

'Don't think you'll find any kiddies to fiddle down there, do you?'

'Sick fucker.'

'Oi, we're talking to you, paedo!'

He heard the rush of air, boot slipping between his feet like a crook. Tarmac pivoted up to smack him in the face. His nose cracked, tongue lanced by a tooth, mouth welling with blood. Carlos coughed, spluttered, rolled onto his side. His broken shades slid off.

'I'm... sorry,' he said. He saw the faces, dimly lit by one of the few streetlamps in this vacant fringe of the city. He could make out their sneers, their abject disgust and hatred.

'He's fucking sorry,' a guy jeered. One of the women grasped his arm, before spitting at Carlos and jabbing his gut with her heel.

'Fucking kids are sorry,' she said. 'Fucked up kids... sick fucking...' She seemed to lose her thread, and gave him another kick to make up for it.

'I'm not him,' Carlos whispered, though he didn't know if he was saying it to his attackers or himself. His mind was loose. A boot thwacked into his eye socket and darkness blotted his vision. Wetness seeped into his side, liquor or blood he didn't know. *I'm not him*, he thought. Meaning, *I'm not that man. I'm not that monster. I'm the icon.*

I'm the King.

SO YOU'VE BEEN CANCELLED

There was nothing quite like the thrill of the cancel.

Not that Oliver White believed in the term 'cancel'. Cancel was just the word bigots cried when they were called out, the whine of the right-wing predator as it succumbed to his moral lances. For Oliver, the internet was the great leveller – no longer could gloating celebs, tax-avoiding millionaires or populist ministers sail through life untouchable, corroding society with their toxic behaviour. Real people – *the* people – could now cut anyone down to size.

Oliver White. Journalist, author, socialist, feminist, anti-fascist. He/him. Rainbow flag. Green heart. Red rose. Black fist.

So read his Twitter bio. He had over 850,000 followers, though he knew many of them were tribal trolls, lurking there only to snap at his every post with crude slander or a homophobic jibe. Every day he would block another thirty or so users. They'd regularly mock him as the

#WhiteKnight for fighting for his causes, unable to wrap their narrow minds around the idea that Oliver could genuinely care about members of society less fortunate than himself, decrying him and his supporters as the 'virtue signalling wokie army'.

'What's eating you tonight?' Max said, handing him a bowl with a wry smile.

Oliver looked up from his phone, frowning, as Max curled up in an armchair with his pasta and switched on the TV. 'Professor at the University of Lincoln,' he said. 'David Salter. He's reposted an article that claims certain tribes in Sub-Saharan Africa have lower intelligence than other populations. Doesn't look like his first foray into "ethnic" science.'

'Racist old white guy?'

Oliver swallowed a chunk of *(organic, local cooperative)* fusilli. 'A racist old white guy in a position of power at a public institution, regularly invited onto the BBC, indoctrinating the next generation of young adults with his bigoted views.'

'He's actually teaching them the racist studies?' Max raised an eyebrow.

'That's not the point.' Oliver sighed. 'The point is people have a right to know the vile ideologies of those in the establishment. I can draw attention to that. I call it out to the university, and ask if that's really who they want representing them. It's not a crime to use the influence I have to call for progress. It's a moral obligation.'

Oliver turned back to his phone, adding to his Salter thread while he ate and Max watched *The One Show*.

Firing off a perfectly barbed tweet was like pronging an arrow into the bullseye. But the real thrill came when the campaigns he was part of burst into the offline world.

Getting blackface-normalising sketch shows dumped from iPlayer or an accused sex pest's memoir scrapped – that was satisfying. Oliver didn't enjoy when an academic got sacked or a disc jockey lost their slot on LBC – at least not on a personal level – but it was necessary for the greater good of society. That was the goal he always had to focus on. And these people were like knotweed; they always found somewhere else to spring up. No one was ever truly 'cancelled'. It had taken him five years to get Sadie Day banned from Twitter, and soon after she made a comeback on TikTok.

The right had become a hydra. The more you cut away at its insidious rhetoric, the more it erupted all around you. Oliver's inbox was bursting with messages from supporters directing him to the latest crime against morality. Nobody's reputation was immune to an unpleasant discovery, even cherished institutions and long dead artists. In the past few months he'd had to call out The National Sewing Society (ableism), Daniel Wilks (domestic abuse apologist) and even Dora the Explorer (racist). You could smell the fear in the air. Who would mark themselves for the cyber-guillotine next?

Oliver scoffed. 'Have you seen this open letter, *In Defence of Free Speech*?'

'No,' Max said, disinterested, taking Oliver's bowl. 'Are you gonna help wash up?'

'They act like they're the ones being attacked. As if a few comments on Twitter stop them pumping out their bile, which is *actually* killing people. Nothing says, "I'm being silenced" like being paid to write about how you're being silenced in a national newspaper.'

'Have I been silenced?'

'What?'

'I asked you to help wash up.'

•

Oliver's allergies always started with a tingle under his tongue, spreading to a furriness around his throat, itching under his arms and inner thighs, before full blown hives, retching and throttled breathing. Being cancelled felt much the same.

First there was a Twitter mention, which he scanned in the microsecond it took to swipe away the notification on his phone: *Always knew Oliver White was an anti-Semite.*

He didn't think anything of it. Baseless smears went with his territory.

But then came the others. A trickle became a stream became a flood.

Absolutely heartbroken and FUMING #OliverWhite.

Liberal elite hypocrite shows his true Jew-hating colours #OliverWhitesOnly.

Guess that explains his Hitler youth haircut #WhitePower.

Oliver clicked. He scrolled. The same image cascaded before his eyes, over and over, one he hadn't seen in over a decade. Aged nineteen, first year of university, fresh-faced, arm round another boy – Anton – who was wearing a Julie Andrews wig and frock. Oliver was dressed as a German soldier.

'What the fuck?' he muttered. Just about to go down into a tube station, he pushed his way back through the grumbling flow of commuters. He put his *(independent, indigenous women-empowering)* coffee down on a wall and rushed out a tweet.

I am NOT and have NEVER BEEN an anti-Semite. I have nothing but respect for the Jewish people.

Even before he could put his phone away, the barbed replies hooked in.

"The Jewish people." Cringing so hard right now.

Bullshit. Bet you enjoyed being a Jew-fucking Nazi.

Oliver felt the air sucked out of his stomach like a punctured balloon. He had to get out of here. He had to get home. The thrum of people gushing down into the tube station filled him with a nauseous dread, so he stumbled away down the street, fingers shaking so much he almost ordered an Uber Pool by mistake.

In the taxi, he got more of the picture. Anton was now a dancer in Berlin; he'd mentioned the story of his partner wearing an SS uniform in passing, as part of a larger conversation about his time in England and his Jewish roots. He hadn't mentioned Oliver's name. But he had said how his partner had wanted to keep the outfit on when they had intercourse that evening. The interview had come out in a German newspaper a few days earlier. Some web sleuths must have made the connection to Oliver and discovered the photograph.

He fired off another tweet.

The personal – and private – image that has been circulating was taken after my boyfriend at the time and I attended a Sound of Music singalong.

His phone dinged immediately.

Did you make him singalong to the German national anthem too?

Heat seared beneath his temples.

Not much of an apology, musical or otherwise.

Hills are alive with the sound of Oliver White's bigotry #cancelled.

Always knew this guy wasn't kosher.

Jew hater.

Leftist scum.

He clasped the phone so tightly in his fist he was surprised it didn't crack. As they pulled up outside his flat, Oliver slammed the taxi door and stormed inside, forgetting to even give the driver a five-star rating.

Screeching along to an old movie doesn't give you the right to abuse minorities, you insensitive ghoul.

Proof the most woke are the most full of shit.

The latch shuddered in his grip as he closed the front door.

For the many not the Jew.

Pop! Oliver jumped. A cork bounced off the ceiling.

'Anniversary tipple?' Max grinned, proudly brandishing a bottle of champagne. He spotted the iPhone clenched in Oliver's hand. 'I saw your name was trending too – double the reason to celebrate!'

Oliver let out a frustrated sigh as he barged past Max. 'And you didn't even bother to check *why* I was trending?'

'I assumed it was your latest article, no?'

Flinging his bag into the corner of the kitchen, Oliver was just about to offer a scathing reply when he found himself face-to-face with a man in chef's whites. He pivoted, scooting Max into a corner of the corridor with a questioning look.

'I booked caterers,' Max whispered. 'I told you. For our anniversary dinner.'

'Shit.'

'Why shit?'

'I have a Twitter mob to deal with tonight.'

'Are you fucking real?'

'Yes, I'm fucking real.'

15

Oliver gave him a kiss. It wasn't returned.

Calls for *The Guardian* to drop him. Petitions for universities to bar him. Old tweets resurrected – criticisms of Israel, support for Corbyn – more 'proof' of his anti-Semitism. Threads unravelled – *This is the *real* problem with Oliver White* – posturing how his rallies to abolish billionaires were thinly veiled conspiracies against a perceived Jewish elite. *Just look how often he attacks Lord Sugar.*

The mob had risen up, hurling fistfuls of horseshit at Oliver, forming a giant pile of steaming excrement under which to suffocate him. He fought his way through the onslaught, posting rebuttals, scathingly critiquing the vilest replies. The ones that stung the most were those from the left, deserting him at the first whiff of imperfection. They'd repost his words as screenshots, thinking he wouldn't be notified and see, or discuss him as *Ol*ver Wh*te* to prevent him searching them out, as if his name were now a slur.

This is why we don't need privileged cis white men speaking up for us.

But occasionally he'd find a vote of support. *Dressing up for a musical is not a crime. Times change. Anti-fascists persecute Oliver White for dressing as a Nazi like... Nazis.*

He'd like each one, his thumb pounding on the heart icon like he was performing CPR.

The chef served them four courses at their kitchen table. Oliver barely ate a bite. Max didn't say a word, glaring at Oliver as he scrolled and scrolled through his phone. Things hadn't been this icy between them since Oliver berated Max for ordering something from Amazon. 'For God's sake,' Oliver muttered, 'everyone goes as a Nazi for *The Sound of Music*. Anton never said anything about being uncomfortable at the time. We were teenagers for fuck's sake.'

'But you did keep the uniform on when you had sex with him,' Max replied, stony faced.

'I don't remember. We'd been partying.' Oliver held his hands up. 'There wasn't anything... it wasn't deliberate.'

Max glared, turned to the chef. 'Thank you, Pierre. That was wonderful. The food, at least.'

As he closed the front door, Max said he was going to bed. 'You can sleep in the spare room,' he added, when Oliver started to follow.

•

He hoped the rage would have subsided by morning. If anything, it had got worse.

One of the favourable tweets he'd liked had come from a notorious Holocaust-denying vlogger, which the mob had picked up on with delight. Pieces had been written up on the story on most news sites, with the *Mail* taking greatest pleasure in mauling Oliver as a racist hypocrite.

He swiftly reposted the article. *I have been called many things – communist, Marxist – but I will never be accused of being a racist. Those close to me, including my partner (who is Black), will tell you I have never uttered a racist word in my life.*

Still the bile continued to spew.

The trouble with Oliver White (A THREAD)...

Here's why Oliver White's 'apology' is problematic | Story by me.

He was prejudiced. Xenophobic. A bully. An abuser. Every attempt to fight back added fuel to the flames.

'Get your face out of that fucking phone.'

17

Oliver snapped back to reality. It was evening. He hadn't noticed Max coming in through the door. And he'd never seen him this incensed.

'What's up?'

'What's up?! I've asked you – I've told you – *explicitly* – not to talk about me online –'

'I haven't, I didn't say anything about you.'

Max held up his hands, flabbergasted. 'You don't even realise, do you? Christ Almighty. Let me spell it out for you.' He read from his own phone. '"My partner, *who is Black"*. Do you have any idea what it's like to be so casually dismissed like that? Do you have any fucking clue how hard I've worked to not be described as "the black guy"? Of course you don't, you privileged white twat. You think a hard life is people saying some mean things about you on the internet. Well guess what, Olly, some people have mean things to deal with in the real fucking world.'

'Uh...' Oliver was stunned. 'I'm sorry, Max.'

'Whatever. Just don't tweet a fucking apology.'

'Wow.' Oliver put down his phone, followed Max into the kitchen. 'You think all I do is tweet?'

'I think everything you say is a fucking tweet. Every sentence you construct is a one-hundred-and-forty-character jibe, targeted to put someone down or assert your own moral authority. You're not interested in nuance or understanding anymore, you just like to snipe at the world from your virtual soapbox.'

'Two hundred and eighty.'

'What?'

'You can have two hundred and eighty characters on Twitter now,' Oliver said.

'Jesus!' Max grabbed himself a beer out of the fridge. 'You want one?'

18

'Am I going to need one?'

Max shrugged and wandered into the lounge. Oliver poured himself a glass of *(biodynamic, refugee-grown)* wine.

'I didn't mean to demean you,' Oliver said, taking a seat on the sofa opposite Max. 'I just had to prove that I'm not the person they're trying to smear me as.'

'And did you do that?'

'Uh… I… maybe. Some people are never going to accept it. We're in a war now, Max, like it or not. The right has mobilised and they're determined to obliterate anyone who tries to stand up to them.'

Max rolled his eyes. 'There you go again. You always have to blame someone else. It's the right, it's the billionaires, it's the Murdoch press, it's structural racism, it's society – it's never even slightly more complicated than that.'

'That's because it's true! They want to keep people in the dark, but we're waking up. I want to *save* people.'

'Is that what you're doing for me? Am I here to fulfil your white saviour fetish, Olly?'

'Fuck off.'

Max sighed, fingers gripping the arms of his chair. 'I admired you, Olly, you know I did. I was taken in by your passion, your boundless sympathy, your need to challenge the status quo no matter the personal cost. But you've changed. That platform has warped your perspective. You think you'll genuinely change the world if your comments get enough likes and retweets, that you'll enlighten a tipping point of the public if you just post enough sharp quips, that you'll build a better society if you can bring down just enough public figures. But that's not the way it works. You're burrowing into an echo chamber, closing your mind

19

with every witty quote tweet… so much you've become the mirror image of the people you used to hate. And you're fuelling an even more extreme opposition.'

Oliver felt his throat swelling. He took a glug of wine, unable to swallow the lump. This was worse than every criticism he got online. Every email calling him a *smug prick* or threat to *paint a baseball bat red with your commie blood*. 'What are you saying?' he asked, not daring to look Max in the eye.

'It's over, Olly.' Max's fingers released their grip on the armchair. 'We're over. I don't want to be around whatever this is anymore.'

Oliver begged. He pleaded. He called and messaged, till he found himself blocked. Cancelled. Alone in the flat, he opened up Twitter and posted.

Congrats to my so-called allies. You cost me my reputation, relationship, numerous speaking gigs and 5k followers. Way to set back our cause, never mind my personal pain. Maybe have some compassion and think before you tweet.

Oliver White settled back on the sofa, cricking his neck, rotating his wrist, ready to eviscerate the replies as they came in.

LION'S TEETH

She wanted to watch the execution. She wanted to stand there, her breath misting the glass as he was strapped, limb by limb, to the table, arms outstretched in a recumbent crucifixion. She wanted to be part of that gathering of morbid onlookers, satiating their desire to witness the moment James Hilbert took the needle and his last convulsion. But flights to Texas were expensive, so Beth couldn't attend that man's final judgement. She was determined not to miss the next.

James Hilbert died a mere nine years after conviction for his crimes. Beth had recognised his photo the instant she clicked onto the article announcing his impending execution. The 'Sorority Slayer' the BBC headline called him, putting the words in quotations as if that distanced the corporation from the lurid moniker it was using to entice hits. Though in this case 'slayer' was a fairly accurate description. James had returned to the States to live with his father after crashing out of school in the UK. Once there he'd made his way through three sorority houses, slipping in at night to carve up and rape every poor girl he could get his hands on, before he was caught. Twenty-two victims in total – fifteen dead, seven survived. One for every year of his despicable existence. His photograph had been everything you expected of such a monster: rake of black hair, pallid skin, soulless eyes, jagged knife-slash of a sneer.

'It's you,' Beth had whispered at the face on her computer screen. Gazing at the mugshot, she lost herself in every pixel of those callous eyes. 'So that's who you are.'

In the month remaining before the execution, Beth devoured every detail of his case. Every report, hearing, trial and appeal. The death sentence had been a shock, given his youth, but understandable, given the lobbying of the grieving college parents. As such a detestable creature, he had no chance of atonement. Death row had one end for James Hilbert, so there was little point prolonging the inevitable. Lethal injection day came, and the Sorority Slayer was no more.

But James was not the only figure creeping out from the darkness of Beth's past. There was another for her to track down.

•

Twenty years earlier, Bethany was chasing butterflies.

Her yellow dress fluttered as she ran through the park's long grass, bees and seeds scattering in her wake. Midday sun set the skin of her bare arms and neck prickling. Bethany's expression was set; she was a child who could smile and frown at the same time when in deepest concentration. She was so engrossed that she didn't realise she had lost sight of her parents. In fact, she almost barrelled head-first into the older boy's legs.

'Careful there,' he said. 'You'll get hurt.'

She gazed up at the speaker. His head was in silhouette, fringed by a golden halo. 'Who are you?' she asked.

'I'm Danny,' he said. He knelt so they were on the same level. His face was kind and boyish, his voice soft.

'How old are you?'

'I'm fifteen. How old are you?'

'I'm seven next week. My name's Bethany.'

'Well, Bethany, it's lovely to meet someone with such a pretty dress.' When Danny smiled, his lips seemed to stretch all the way round to both ears. 'Do you like flowers, Bethany?'

She shrugged.

'The pretty flowers that the bugs like to smell?'

'I s'pose,' she said. 'Why?'

'I like those flowers a lot. I can show you some that are quite lovely. Perhaps we can find one for your birthday. Would you like that?'

Bethany considered for a moment. She liked birthday presents. She nodded.

Together they walked across the park, over a ridge and down a slope. Danny stopped to point out various plants and trees. 'Ah now you see the dandelion?' he said, pointing to the yellow spouting weed. 'That's one of my favourites. Can you believe that this yellow flower turns into the pinwheel seed head?'

Bethany didn't understand. Danny looked around, before plucking a stalk from the ground. It ended in a ball of white tips. He passed it to her.

'That used to be the flower?' she asked.

'Yes. Why don't you give it a blow?'

Bethany knew what to do. She puffed and sent the dozens of seeds dancing out across the field.

'Well done!' Danny said. 'You've just planted lots of new little dandelion flowers. Shall I tell you where that name comes from?' He began to lead her on through the grass, towards a cluster of trees. 'It comes from the French *dent de lion* – tooth of the lion. Not because of the golden mane of the petals, but the jagged leaves, sharp like vicious teeth!' Sunlight faded as they sank into the gloom of the trees. Bethany plodded behind the boy, her plimsols crunching old foliage. She glanced back to see a last glimpse of the sunny park, lit like a painting in a dark gallery, before it was extinguished by branches.

'Where are we going?'

Danny looked down at her and smiled. That lovely smile, pinned by two perfect dimples. 'I'm taking you to meet my friend,' he said, as they reached a small clearing. 'Here he is now.'

The boy waiting there, looking a little older than Danny, did not seem so friendly. He had on a black hoodie and jeans torn open at the knees. His gaze seared from under heavy dark eyebrows, seeming to assess her before he nodded to Danny. He stepped forward as Danny nudged her closer. Reaching out, he took hold of her hands. 'You're a mucky pup, aren't you?' He had an accent like in the movies on TV. He started picking flakes of grub from her palms.

'I want to go now,' Bethany said, but it seemed to come out as a question, an appeal for permission.

The boy took it as such, shaking his head. 'Close your eyes.'

Danny had a hand resting on her shoulder. She looked up at him. 'Go on, Bethany,' he said, with his smile. 'It's best to keep your eyes closed.'

When it was done, they told her that she should keep her mouth shut as well as her eyes. Pushed away from the clearing, she stumbled through the woods blind, too scared to peek and see where she was going. Even when she made it out into the sunshine, she kept her eyes shut. And when her parents found her, she was too scared to tell them where she'd been. In fact, she barely spoke for months.

•

That picture of James in the article, older but unmistakeably the dark-haired boy in the woods, proved a catalyst for recollection. Memories buried, like a half-forgotten dream, began to resurface. Coalescing into a firm enough form for her mind to grasp as reality. She remembered what had happened to her in the park all those years before. What they had done to her.

Beth started to investigate. James Hilbert was reported on, convicted and despatched, but the one who led her into the woods remained a mystery. She had only a first name and an image of the boyish youth in her mind. While watching James's case conclude from a distance, Beth trawled the internet for clues. She started with the area local to where she used to live in Bradford, searching for any news articles from the time mentioning crimes, teens, 'Daniel's or nearby schools. It took persistence, but Beth had never lost her childhood determination.

Her first breakthrough came from the *Bradford Post* website. Squashed in between adverts, pop ups and videos was a story about a group of students at Undercliffe Secondary. They were completing a memorial garden for a year seven girl called Ellen Wren, who had passed away from an asthma attack on the way home from school.

Pictured beside a newly planted tree were the students, including the fresh-faced bolt from her past – named in the caption as Daniel Galpin, who had been able to source plants for the project from the garden centre where he worked on weekends.

Once she had a name, it was much easier to glean further information. With the right searches, she could unearth countless PDFs and documents the school had left lying about online – newsletters, parent bulletins, school trip details, lists of grades and graduations. One such piece gave her the shock that James Hilbert attended the same school, though a year above Daniel. Beth supposed it was no surprise that Undercliffe had tried to scrub that titbit from their record.

There were a few more local news stories on the girl, Ellen Wren. While she'd long suffered from asthma, her parents had raised some concerns about the tragedy. Apparently she'd been found in a wooded area behind the school, which they claimed she never walked through. But no one, it seemed, had followed up on this.

Sourcing all she could on the school, the garden centre and that area of town, she learned that Daniel had grown up in a foster home. Most records were not available online, but there were snatches of activity she could grasp from old social media posts. It seemed Daniel had never published anything on such accounts himself (or at least they had been deleted), but he was occasionally featured in those of someone else. After finishing school, he'd gone to university in Essex to study horticulture.

Details became scant since then. It took Beth endless midnight hours hunched over her laptop to dredge up any more nuggets. Once he'd moved into adulthood, employment, across the country, records or mentions were

26

thin on the ground. A Facebook post showed him joining the team of a ground maintenance company near Sheffield. They never mentioned him again. A report on a pub brawl in Manchester named a Daniel Galpin as a witness, but she couldn't be sure it was the same man. Every hint of his name online triggered a Google alert to her inbox, and eventually she caught him. On the Instagram feed for Rowley Chilli Farm, planting up some pots for Valentine's hampers only the week before. Beth checked the map. Burnley. He'd returned home.

Daniel was now twenty years older than the boy she'd met in the park. He was a man of thirty-five. Beth, a grown woman herself. On a bitter February evening, she parked up outside Rowley Farm. After a quick visit to the onsite shop, she returned to her car and waited for closing time.

•

It wasn't a long drive to the Dales. Her tyres trundled over course ground, her lights picked up flashes of heather as she travelled further into the wilderness. When she judged the distance from civilisation far enough, she pulled to a halt, regarding herself in the rear-view mirror. The old determined frown. She smiled. A jolt and a thump from the back of the vehicle. Her passenger must be waking up.

A familiar thrill pulsed through her, but she kept a steady grip on her nerves. The chase was always fun, but this was a day of reckoning. It was too personal to squander.

Taking one last steadying breath, she got out of the driver's seat, circled the car and popped open the boot. Daniel Galpin stared up at her. The round baby face was still present, but his flesh was yellow in the pallid boot light,

27

limbs contorted into the small enclosure – bare feet twisted behind him, wrists strapped together with a cable tie. Beth had stripped his torso down to a thin vest. She found people more compliant when they were cold.

'Hello, Danny,' she said.

When he struggled to reply, she removed the damp grey socks stuffed in his mouth and tossed them aside. 'Wuh… wuh… what the hell is happening?' he said. To be fair to him, basic comprehension was hard with his head still bleeding from the knockout blow she'd delivered in the car park.

'You don't remember me?'

'No… What do you want? Do you want money?'

'I want to remind you about the things you used to get up to with James Hilbert.'

His eyes widened, jaw set in fear.

'You remember *him*, don't you?' Beth said. 'Maybe there were others too.'

'I… I didn't –'

'Ellen Wren, do you remember her?'

He started to shake, an uncontrollable shudder she found repulsive.

'I see you do. Well I don't care about what you and James did to her, or what you might've done to any other girls –'

'I haven't – not since – I was going through a lo–'

Beth held up a hand to silence him. 'I don't care about them. I'm here for me. We might not be so different, Danny boy. I like catching things too. That's what I was doing when you caught me.' She turned her palms over, recollecting the smeared flakes of butterfly wings – *mucky pup* – that James had picked off. 'You caught me in the park, when I was only a little girl enjoying the sunshine. You told me about the flowers, which you really do like, don't you, Danny? The lion's teeth. Well, when a real lion has you in its teeth, it doesn't let you go. It will maul you for hours.'

His shudder intensified. 'I'm so sorry,' he blubbered.

Beth grinned at him, though hers was cold. She'd never been able to master the comforting envelop of Danny's smile. 'You told me to close my eyes. To keep them shut nice and tight and it would all be over. You watched while he grabbed me, and bit me, and grabbed himself. You made me walk away from the disgusting things he did with my eyes shut, not knowing if I would ever make it back into the sun.' She placed a hand round the side of his face. 'You're going to close your eyes now, Danny.'

Shaking his head, his gaze pleaded with her. 'No, I'm sorry… no...'

'I thought you might say that,' she replied. 'Lucky I made a trip to your shop then.' From her back pocket she plucked a pair of latex gloves and stretched them on, enjoying his wince as the material snapped against her wrists. Out of her jacket pocket came the little jar. 'You know about the Carolina Reaper, of course. One of your farm's specialities. Hottest pepper in the world, they told me.' She showed him the label on the jar of chilli paste. 'More than two hundred times more intense than a jalapeno. Spicy stuff!'

She popped off the lid. Scooped out a finger of paste with one hand. Swooped in to clasp Daniel's face with the other. And coated his eyeball. His screams were guttural. They echoed across the deserted scrubland. His body writhed in its tight confines. But Beth was strong. She held him firm, pinning back the lids to smear paste into every corner of his eyes. When she was done, she tossed the jar aside along with the gloves, flipped out a penknife and cut through the cable tie at his wrists.

Daniel didn't seem to notice. Choking through the screams, crimson tears doused his smooth cheeks, snot hucking from his nostrils and spit flying with every cry. As Beth wrenched him from the boot, he opened his eyes for just a moment – two red orbs in the moonlight – before screeching from the pain and clamping them shut.

'That's right, Danny,' Beth said. 'Keep your eyes closed. It's for the best. Just keep them closed, and walk away.'

He staggered forwards, bare arms swinging wildly, but she dodged aside. Any words were lost in sobs. His naked toes crunched over bracken; they'd be punctured raw, and blue from the winter night in a matter of hours. Beth watched him for a moment, swaying and howling like Frankenstein's scarecrow, before closing the boot and slipping back into her car. Daniel swung round as she revved up the engine, hobbling after her, but there was no chance of catching up. After cranking the heating up to a toasty embrace, Beth gave him a final glance in the mirror and switched on the radio. Nothing like a bit of smooth jazz to cleanse the avenging soul.

THE KING IS DEAD, PART II

15th July 2017. Palm Beach, Florida.

Sunrise sparkled on the Atlantic. Pinpricks almost too bright to look at dotted the waves. Pleasure boats out for an early cruise glided along the horizon. Diamond DaSilva watched the seascape from her balcony, taking a ragged drag on her morning cigarette. She didn't smoke much, but when she did, she smoked hard. This July had been a forty-a-day month.

'Fuck it,' she said, stubbing out her cig on the railing and tossing it over into the swimming pool. Harry would fish it out, when she allowed him back to work. The beach house had been on skeleton staff since Diamond took herself into lockdown: Vi to help with the cooking, Norma popping in to clean and do the laundry, her friend Jess for occasional company. But her nights were lonely. So many empty rooms. She lay in bed, too restless to sleep, gazing out the full height windows, watching the wind lash the barricade of palm trees enclosing the property. Sometimes she felt the urge to get up and run through those windows, leap from the balcony and dash her bones against the trees.

But she didn't. And in the morning, the sun came, dazzling bright as ever.

Diamond stalked along the balcony, which wrapped around the entire upper floor of the house. At the front of the building she observed vans pulling into the driveway, television crew spilling out as her manager, Karen, marched over to herd them inside.

And there was Marcia Halliday, star of *Mornings with Marcia* and the so called 'Mother of America', who had held the country to her ample bosom for thirty years. She was network TV royalty and barely glanced at the house before slipping on her shades and striding alongside her crew. Diamond mused what it might be like to have a mother like Marcia. Her own mother was a painter, though more well known for being a descendent of European royalty. Diamond hadn't seen her since she was a child. The woman had cut herself off from everything associated with Dante – including their daughter – after their short-lived marriage ended in divorce.

Not that Diamond cared. She felt no attachment to her mother; she'd always seen herself as a daddy's girl. DaSilva through and through. Heiress to the King. Dante had given her everything – a fairy-tale childhood of global tours, shopping sprees, extravagant parties and, of course, their own castle to call home. He'd been everything to her. Since he'd passed, Diamond had cut her own way to success, using her Disney sitcom as a springboard to a teen pop career.

The patio door slid open. 'Makeup,' Adam said.

Diamond sighed and followed her head of PR inside. Esme gave her a timid smile as she guided her into the swivel chair, tucked a paper collar round her neck and began applying foundation. Old aches crawled up her spine.

Endless hours sitting in front of a mirror while people poked at her with brushes, tweezers and curlers was not something she'd missed in her time away from the spotlight.

'Am I pretty, Esme?' she asked.

The young woman smiled again. 'The prettiest, sweetie.'

Karen barged into the room. 'Do you have the record?' she asked Adam. As he pressed the vinyl into her hands, they shared a furtive exchange.

Diamond roiled. She couldn't bear to look at the album cover, a bland monochrome image of her face, repurposed from an old publicity shoot. She'd been preparing for a surprise drop of this record, a passion project, her most personal work to date, when the scandal had hit. Adam had called for an immediate rebrand. 'Thank Christ we hadn't gone public with *that* title,' he'd said over the phone.

'That title was my truth!' Diamond had cried in return. 'I spent my fourteen-day silent retreat nurturing those words!'

But the label had insisted. A Diamond DaSilva album called *LOVE CHILD* was not acceptable 'in the current climate'. Not only had the title been scrapped, but they ordered a 'soft rebrand' of Diamond herself. Her surname would be dropped, ushered in by the record's new name – *I Am Di*.

Adam scratched his pretentious goatee. 'So they agreed?'

Karen nodded. 'No mention of KOC' – meaning King of Cool, a taboo seeming to have arisen even around Dante's moniker – 'but, of course, the interview's live…'

'Live or not, if they bring him up, our lawyers will be hounding them to an early grave. Sorry, Di.'

33

Diamond exhaled, swatting Esme's brush away. 'You can at least say my dad's name. You can mention him in *my house*. He *existed* for fuck's sake!'

'Honey, we're only trying to protect you,' Karen said.

'You're only trying to protect your careers. Which my dad built for you.'

'Yes, and my career is protecting your career,' Adam said. 'This is an extremely delicate situation in an extremely volatile climate, which we've been working our asses off to defuse.'

Diamond rolled her eyes. This was exactly the kind of reaction she detested. The complicity of people to believe any story and instantly disregard her father's decades of achievement and charity, to erase him from history, enraged her. After the stories first came out, she'd been astounded at the willingness of the public to lap them up like they were the goddamn gospel, but in the month since, she'd become more jaded. People wanted an easy-to-swallow narrative, to see their heroes cut small, banish them as a monster and believe that would solve all the world's problems.

'You never… you didn't… with Dad?' Diamond had asked Jess deep into a long night on the wine in her first week of isolation.

'Not once,' Jess had replied emphatically. She grasped Diamond's hand. 'People will make up any old shit for airtime, Di.'

And Dante's accusers had certainly got airtime. The documentary, newspaper interviews, slots on talk shows… there were rumours one was even planning to publish a memoire. They must have made a fortune from raping her dead father's name. Those cowards even waited till he'd been in the ground for a decade before coming in to attack.

34

What made it all so sickening was how much Dante had cared for children throughout his life. Diamond had seen it all growing up: grand parties lavished on hundreds of youngsters, free reign to play in the Castle, endless gifts, tour passes, dancing on stage. He had believed that every kid deserved to be treated like a prince or princess.

But, despite her management's intentions, Diamond was not yet prepared to let her family legacy sink into the mud without a fight. During her solitude, she had made a few calls. There was another side to this story to tell. *Dante: The Truth* was the working title. She would narrate, Jess had agreed to be interviewed and Scott Hendrix, with whom she'd collaborated on multiple music videos, was interested in directing. They'd find a photography expert who could prove the infamous images were fake. They'd get Netflix on board. She was sure of it.

'Are you going to behave?' Adam asked.

Staring at his smug, idiotic face, Diamond realised the depths of her hatred for the man.

'Let's get on with it,' she said.

Downstairs, she greeted Marcia Halliday with air kisses to both cheeks. She let the sound men mic her up and Esme make final adjustments to her face. 'All set? How are you feeling today?' Marcia asked.

'I'm good,' Diamond replied, without feeling.

'Well you look stunning, Di.'

'Thank you.' Diamond noted the abbreviated use of her name, something she supposed she'd have to get used to hearing in public now. She took her seat in a fold out director's chair across from Marcia, both of them blazoned by portable lights. Her gaze wandered across the pool, the water rippling in gentle waves. She wished she knew how to swim.

Marcia coughed, exchanged a few words with the crew. 'Just a minute now,' she said.

Diamond straightened her back like she'd been taught, raising her chin to catch the best light and soften any shadows. Marcia nodded, then turned to the camera over Diamond's shoulder, her all-American wattage flaring in an instant.

'Welcome. I'm Marcia Halliday and you're watching *Mornings with Marcia*. You join me today in Palm Beach, where I've been fortunate enough to be invited to spend some time with superstar pop sensation Diamond DaSilva in her lovely home.'

Diamond caught sight of Adam and Karen cringing in her peripheral. She knew they'd instructed the TV people to only refer to her as Di.

'Hello.' Marcia turned to her, all warm fuzzy smiles. 'Diamond DaSilva. How does hearing that name make you feel now?'

Chewing over the question, Diamond gazed past Marcia, across the cluster of her parasites. Adam looked like he was about to have a hernia, or rugby tackle Marcia into the pool. Only Jess made eye contact with her, a beautiful, compassionate connection that took her back across the crazy years of their childhood and gave her the strength to reply.

'How does it make me feel?' She smiled. 'The same as it always has, Marcia. It makes me feel proud.'

DEEP STATE

You know the word.

Margot did. She supposed some part of her, dormant, always had. Now that part had awakened, and Margot was volcanic. Her calling had found her. Her time had come.

Fingers tightening on the blender, choking the handle. The blades revved up.

The day is almost here.

And Margot was ready.

MARCH 2020

While not quite as momentous as Diana or the Twin Towers, the tubby blonde's address to the nation, announcing the greatest constraints on civil liberty in British history from behind a desk in the corner of his Downing Street office, would be forever pressed into the memory of the country, a pushpin in the collective cranium. And beneath the initial shock, Margot Kyle felt a stirring of unease, that perhaps this moment might just prove to be a tragedy on the scale of a dead princess or demolished skyscrapers.

Unprecedented, that was what they said. What everyone kept saying.

But they were talking about the virus they claimed was sweeping the globe. About the decisive actions of a quasi-wartime government. No one was talking about the unprecedented loss of freedom that was blanketing the country like overnight snow. That didn't get a mention.

Following the Prime Minister's broadcast, Margot drove straight to work. The business park where the Kyle Centre was located was dead. She swiped her fob to pass through sliding glass doors into the fitness studio she had owned for over fifteen years. Flicking a switch, she turned on the central strip of lights. She surveyed her studio, cold and sallow in the half-light; exercise mats, stacks of yoga blocks, balls and hand weights neatly stacked to the sides.

A decade-and-a-half of building her business up from nothing. This studio, only here because of her perseverance. A second home for its hundreds of members, shuttered. All this equipment, set to gather dust. The livelihoods of her team of instructors, cut like the string of a balloon.

'Utter insanity,' she whispered.

APRIL

The world had cracked. On TV, an endless barrage of viral fear. Husband, holed up in his study, working even longer hours than before. Kids, deprived of their basic right to education. Cleaner and gardener, unable to perform their contracted duties. Someone had to be responsible for all this. Someone had to be held to account.

What staggered Margot was how willingly the public surrendered their freedom and accepted this authoritarian regime. How could a nation built on liberty discard it so freely? The economy was collapsing faster than an overwhipped soufflé, and no one seemed to be worried about what this would mean for generations of young workers. Even when she tried to talk to Derek about it, he shut her down with a pat 'We've just got to focus on protecting the NHS right now.'

Margot knew she had to act. She applied for business loans, furloughed her staff on 80% pay (leaving them no doubt free to enjoy the spring break while she fretted about their future) and chipped in to a multimillionaire's crowdfunded lawsuit against the government's egregious lockdown.

Derek was content working from home, coding away from dawn till dusk at his screen. Their seven-year-old twins, Miles and Giles, relished the break from school. They raced around the family's renovated farmhouse, playing in the sprawling gardens and their swimming pool. Their private school delivered classes, which they grudgingly tuned into on their iPads, before switching to Minecraft as soon as the teacher signed off.

With the mainstream media trotting out nothing but state-sponsored scaremongering, Margot wondered if anyone out there was speaking the truth. She logged into the Kyle Centre's Twitter account to post another apology that the studio had been forced to close.

Her eyes drifted to the trending topics. She clicked on the top one: Lizzie Sayles. A woman in her late twenties, attractive, causing outrage for her video celebrating a garden centre which had stayed open despite the lockdown.

'What are we supposed to do if we can't garden?' Lizzie exclaimed. 'Stay indoors? Plants can't spread a virus! You don't see flowers making people cough and sneeze! I for one applaud this place for showing some common sense and staying open, and I applaud every person who's rejected government tyranny to come out here today.'

Margot was stunned. Most of the commentary around Lizzie Sayles was vitriol, but she ignored this, clicking into the woman's profile and skimming through her tweets. She seemed to be posting the same thoughts that had been swimming round Margot's head, crystallising her feelings of unease into sharp, impactful statements.

Fear is more contagious than Covid, and probably more deadly.

Democracy dies when good people don't stand up to authoritarianism.

Has anyone actually seen 'the science'???

Margot scrolled, and scrolled, for most of that afternoon. She watched Lizzie's videos. She digested the articles Lizzie posted. She sought the outspoken experts Lizzie quoted. And soon she started to get an idea of what was really going on.

MAY

An email from one of her instructors, listed in her contacts as 'Kickbox': Could the Kyle Centre start running Zoom fitness classes?

Margot almost choked on her coffee.

This is your chance. Show him the truth.

She started hammering her reply into her keyboard, copying in the rest of the team.

The Kyle Centre is built on expertise and personalised – IN PERSON – training sessions. I will not risk damaging my reputation with substandard 'virtual' classes because of draconian restrictions enforced upon us by this corrupt government. I am glad you want to get back to work (which doesn't seem to be too common a trait in your generation!!) but if you all want to have a job in 6 months, I recommend you get out on the streets and protest this illegal lockdown!!

Send.

Margot thought for a moment, then realised she could share more about what she'd discovered over the past weeks.

If you're interested in what's really going on behind 'the science', I suggest doing a bit of research. Doesn't seem to be much real consensus around this Covid virus (many say no worse than flu or common cold). Only handful of deaths in under 60s. Any of you think it's very worrying that they want to trash the economy, children's education and mental health of millions for a disease with a 0.01% mortality rate??

She attached links to various articles that explored the doubts around the story pushed by politicians and mainstream media, as well as a fascinating six-hour YouTube presentation from Professor Lawrence Dillinger, detailing the connection between current events and the long, silently waged 'war on capital and individual freedom'.

Margot closed her laptop, taking a slurp of coffee as she watched the boys chasing each other across their sloping lawns. A bitter thought pricked her like a wasp sting.

What future will your boys have after all this?
Margot opened up her laptop, jumping onto Twitter.

JUNE

'You're not seriously going to wear that are you?' Margot asked. 'You look like you've hooked a pair of Y-fronts over your ears.'

'It's the law,' came Derek's muffled reply from behind his facemask.

Margot scoffed. 'And that's exactly why I've been telling you we need to worry.'

'It's just a mask.' He folded up the piece of cloth. 'We only have to wear it in the supermarket.'

'You can wear it in the supermarket. I certainly won't be. It may be "just a mask" in Waitrose this week, but give it a year and we'll all be marched to labour camps in burqas.'

Derek, laughing, 'You don't really believe that.' More hesitantly, 'Do you...?'

Margot shrugged. 'Who knows what they'll do anymore? We're letting them rule by whim, without even any parliamentary debate.'

'Margot, you know it's an emergency situation…'

'You can say that again. Sometimes it feels like I'm the only one treating all this like an emergency.'

But that wasn't strictly true. Over the past couple of weeks, Margot had become an active member of free-face advocacy group Mums Against Masks, which she'd joined on Facebook. While lamestream journalists were falling over themselves to offer 'homemade face covering' demos and virtue-signalling lefties were posting masked selfies on

Instagram, the members of MAM were sharing plenty of interesting ideas in one of the few places where open debate was still permitted.

Margot had forwarded on some of the studies posted in the group, from academics across the globe, showing how mask-wearing actually *harmed* the immune system and made people *more susceptible* to viral infection.

'I'm not sure I believe this Professor Dillinger bloke,' Derek had said. 'Where's his credentials?'

'Where's anyone's credentials?' Margot had snapped back. 'The internet is rife with fake news the government wants us to believe, all so we'll go along with their agenda. I mean, it's crazy that people aren't questioning anything anymore. The state wants to keep us all locked up, but they're happy for hordes of black people to flood the streets protesting against statues. What's that about?'

Margot knew what the masks and the lockdowns and the 'social distancing' were really about. They wanted to stop people communicating. Eliminate free speech. Suppress dissent.

Not on her watch.

JULY

Things were looking up. Finally, her cleaner had agreed to return (though insisted on opening all the windows 'for ventilation' faster than Margot could get them shut). The Kyle Centre was allowed to welcome members again. Mums Against Masks had become a more supportive community than any Margot had been a part of in the offline world. And the more sensible papers – *The Mail*, *The*

Telegraph, *The Spectator* – were even beginning to publish some lockdown scepticism.

But it wasn't long before mutterings of discontent from her team about a lack of 'Covid security' at the studio.

'What's the problem?' she ranted to Derek. 'I've done the risk assessment' – all the staff were under 40, so not at risk from the virus, according to her interpretation of the data – 'and shelled out for an industrial sized bottle of anti-bac. They're all adults. Our members are adults. Everyone can make their own common-sense decision about whether they want to come in, keep their body and mind healthy, or face the consequences of a ruined economy and no employment.'

'You told them that? In those words?'

'Of course I bloody told them that! And do you know what they said?'

'What?'

'The body pump girl suggested we do those bloody *Zoom fitness classes* again. As long as this is *my* company, it is *my* name above the door' – at this point Margot had pointed to The Kyle Centre logo, which was indeed above the door – 'we will not be damaging my brand and sacrificing my integrity with *Zoom fitness classes*.'

'And what did she say to that?'

'She said she's got an offer from Peloton.'

AUGUST

You have to take a stand. They may scorn you, mock you and fear you, but you have to fight this oppression. History will vindicate you.

44

Margot took the train into London, anticipation thrumming through her veins. As the city approached, she began to spot others en route to the same destination – those rejecting the mask mandate, those with badges and signs: *I am a free man! State control is the real virus! Hang up on 5G!*

'All viruses are killed by direct sunlight,' she informed the masked and disgruntled woman she'd sat beside, straightening the *Save Old Normal* t-shirt she'd ordered from Lizzie Sayles' Etsy store.

The bubbles of nerves she'd felt upon leaving had swelled to excitement. She was doing the right thing. She was part of something. A community. A movement.

Trafalgar Square. Hundreds of bodies had engulfed the roads, too many for the (thought) police to even attempt to oppose. A makeshift stage had been erected, focusing the crowd's attention.

'Make some noise! Make a *frenzy*!' the compere shouted into his mic, to riotous cheers. 'For Mr Bert Colbert!'

A hefty middle-aged man in leather biker gear took to the stage. Margot was shocked to see his sprawling copper beard clasped back by a blue medical mask. The crowd seemed similarly stunned, their clapping petering out. Bert Colbert grasped the microphone, unhooked the mask with that hand, and sparked up a lighter with the other.

'We will not be muzzled!' he bellowed, touching the flame to the mask, which crinkled into a pathetic smoky ball. A white wave of white applause tore through the crowd. Margot found herself yelling and screaming in delight along with those around her. One man was so enthusiastically jumping up and down that he knocked into a mother in front of him, sloshing his can of lager all over her cradled infant.

'The day is coming, my friends,' Colbert continued. He left a gap between every sentence, which was punctuated by more cheering. 'The people are rising. *We* the people. The Frenzy. We will fight for our freedom. We will fight for the truth. We will fight against the state's tyrannical agenda!'

A skinhead beside her was wearing a shirt emblazed with the slogan *2020=1984.* 'It's pure Orwell,' he said. '*1984, Animal Farm* and *Brave New World* all rolled into one.'

'Just look at it: Covid-19,' added a woman swaddled in a parka. 'They're not even trying to hide that it's the nineteenth version of the virus manufactured by China.'

Margot had heard about the #FreeTheTruth protest through Mums Against Masks, but from chatting with her awakened comrades, she now knew that word had spread through a dozen other forums and messaging apps. All kinds of people were coming together, and they stripped the scales even further from Margot's eyes.

Dots were joined, connections made, at lightning speed.

Virus lab – lockdown – control – new normal – new world order – great reset – united nations – masked singer – masked population – six feet apart – military protocol – public suppression – elite cabal – child abductions – secret experiments – underground tunnels – 5G – 9/11 – BLM – MKUltra – mass vaccinations – microchips – the deep state.

On the train home Margot sought out Bert's podcast, *Truth Watch.* He'd been posting hour-long daily episodes since the start of the plandemic, and she began devouring them at once. Over the next week she paced the garden, AirPods in, Colbert raging in her ears. Every time the boys or Derek tried to get her attention, she waved them away. No time for distractions.

Besides, they weren't interested in listening to her views anymore, so why should she give them the time of day?

'They call us crazy,' Colbert said, in a rare sombre moment. 'They always call people like us crazy. But you must remember that's just an attempt to discredit us, to make us *feel* crazy. If you look at the original Roman meaning of the word *frenzy*, it refers to a heightened state of understanding. That's its true meaning. So when we are *frenzied*, we are awakened. We see the reality behind the delusion. Our Day of Frenzy will come when enough of us are awake. Friends, that day is coming.'

Colbert laid out the truth of what was happening, and what they had to do about it.

SEPTEMBER

The truth was more disturbing than anything Margot could have envisaged. But it made a nightmarish sort of sense. Once all the pieces started to click into place, the grim picture was sharp.

Nothing that had transpired this year was accidental. It was just the bursting blister of a conspiracy that had been bubbling away below the surface for years, possibly decades. The deeper Margot dug, beyond Facebook, far into the subreddits and 8kun message boards, the closer she got to the truth.

Thousands of children had been going missing each year, and a team of dedicated online sleuths had uncovered evidence that the abductions were all linked. Infants were being taken across the globe to be abused and experimented on by a sinister group intent on engineering a way to control the population en mass. Naturally, it was only a matter of time before corrupt governments had colluded with these monsters, and so the deep state had been infiltrated. Its tendrils were vast, turning many across all levels of society into enablers, fuelling and concealing their crimes. And now their silent war was upon us, with every weapon of fear and control in use to cripple the public into submission.

You know the word.

Yes, Margot knew. The word was *frenzy*, and the moment she'd heard it uttered by Colbert it had connected with her. The frenzied, the truth-seekers, the resistance. She was part of something great.

So Margot stewed alone, hidden away from her family in the conservatory with only her laptop for company. She didn't go into the studio, leaving Kickbox and Pilates to run the day-to-day of the business. The Kyle Centre had haemorrhaged clients, which some of the instructors still blamed on a lack of online classes, but Margot put down to a sleepwalking public cowed by fear. Even Derek had had the cheek to tell her she should be worried about the company and her income more than her 'silly conspiracies', but he spent most of his time now with his study door shut, muffling the rumble of endless phone calls.

Look at them.

Margot gazed out the kitchen window at her boys, as she prepared their lunchtime soup. Miles and Giles were laughing, spraying the gardener with their supersoakers, leaping over the flowerbeds, bombing into the pool. They were so young, so untainted, so vulnerable.

Just think what could happen to them without you.

Her fingers went ghostly white as she gripped the hand blender. She looked down at the pan of vegetables and bore down with the gadget, relishing as chunks were crushed and masticated by her blades.

OCTOBER

With the government continuing to screw the country over with forever shifting tiers and local restrictions, Margot called all her staff into the studio for a crisis meeting.

'These are dark days indeed,' she said, voice thick with horror as she glared at each person in turn – Kickbox, Pilates, Yoga, Spin, Zumba, Meditation, Tai Chi, Dumbbell and the new Body Pump. 'This fascist government is determined to crush the economy. They'll have you all out on the streets unless we start getting more members in. No more reduced occupancy classes. No frozen contracts. I need you going door-to-door flyering if that's what it takes to get people in here.'

Now they were beginning to reflect a spectre of her fear, glancing nervously at each other and trying to edge into the corners of the cramped office as Margot paced between them. Perhaps they were starting to wake up at last.

The next day Tai Chi sent an email round the office saying that he had tested positive for Covid. Before Margot could react, Kickbox had responded to tell everyone that they would have to self-isolate and close the Kyle Centre for ten days.

Fury seared up to her temples.

Absolutely not!! she typed, fingers jabbing the keys through the base of the laptop. *We are on our knees as it is! If we close the business will go under!*

Message sent, she took a stuttering breath, then dived straight into another.

You do not have to self-isolate. He probably just had a cold. These tests are notoriously inaccurate – there are many lawsuits against them across the world. That's why we're in this casedemic. Leading scientists have discredited PCR tests. Here she posted links to articles on Lawrence Dillinger's blog. *Look at the law!! You do not have to isolate unless you came within 2 metres of him, which none of you should have under the guidelines.* (Margot didn't think it worth mentioning that their meeting had been held in a room barely two metres wide.) *You didn't have to come in for the meeting if you didn't feel safe. You were free to make your own decisions! The survival of this business and your jobs depends on common sense and not submitting to the tyranny of test and trace!*

'You're not actually sending that, are you?' Derek had been reading over her shoulder.

'Of course I am,' Margot said, to the whoosh of the email departing. 'Someone has to stand up to this nonsense.'

Derek sighed, ran a hand through his thinning hair.

'I know you don't agree with me,' Margot said. 'That's fine. But when did it become a crime to be sceptical?'

'That's not what this is about.'

'Oh, it's exactly what it's about,' she snapped. 'You're so smug, believing what you're told, but I have news for you, Derek. The truth is coming out. And no amount of censorship is going to stop me –'

'This is about your responsibility as a business owner. As an employer.'

'I've been the only one trying to defend their jobs throughout this whole year!'

'You're putting your staff at risk. You're encouraging, and pressuring, them to take risks, while dangling their continued employment – in the middle of a global pandemic – over their heads. Even if, for whatever reason, you don't believe the virus is real –'

'Shut up!' Margot cried, furious now. 'If you would even look at the data – the *true* figures – you'd see what a sham this all is. Then you'd understand what the state is really trying to do. How do you think they want to end this mess? Mass vaccinations? Yeah, I think we know what's really in those injections.'

Derek took a steadying breath and Margot realised he was barely containing an anger rivalling her own.

'Your arrogance is staggering,' he said, incredulous. 'You claim to be a sceptic, to be out-thinking the rest of the population, but you'll happily lap up any codswallop spewed out by those crackpots you follow.'

'Pah! You people only call them crackpots because they dare to challenge mainstream groupthink.'

'I call them crackpots because they are, objectively, fucking crackpots. You know why they're doing it?' Derek jabbed a finger at her *Free Britain Now* sweatshirt. 'To sell you t-shirts. That "Professor" Dillinger? I looked him up. He was sacked from his only teaching post in the nineties. But his YouTube videos are racking up views in the hundreds of thousands, and each one is packed with advertising. Bert Colbert's podcast – it's sponsored. He's banking speaking gigs by the dozen as a "professional contrarian". They're con artists, Margot. Nothing but con artists, taking advantage of a confusing situation to make a quick buck.'

Margot glared at him. 'Well, I believe in free speech. And believe *me*, you'll miss it once it's gone.'

He sighed again. 'Free speech doesn't give anyone the right to shout "Bomb!" in a crowded airport, and it doesn't give them the right to pump out dangerous misinformation in the midst of a deadly pandemic.'

An icy silence, broken only by the ticking of the kitchen clock.

'Are we done?' Margot said.

In the hallway, clattering as Miles and Giles came in from the garden, bare feet smacking on tiles, breathless laughter.

'Come back to us, Margot,' Derek said, more gently now. 'Don't put them at risk. Come back to reality.'

He placed a hand on top of hers. She shook it off.

Five days later, he started to complain about a migraine.

'It's just a headache,' she told him.

Then he got a cough.

'It's just a cold,' she said.

And then he retired to bed, breathless.

'Flu,' she decided.

NOVEMBER

You've always known.

Margot's eyes snapped open on hydraulic springs. Staring up at the dark ceiling, revulsion to the realisation flooded through her. The man breathing raggedly beside her, the man she'd been married to for twenty years, the man

52

who'd fathered her beloved boys, had been scheming to sell those children into abuse and horrific experimentation all this time.

Silent tears from unblinking eyes cut her cheeks. Her head burned as she examined the idea, turning it over, and as it rolled, like a snowball, it gathered mass and momentum. His endless hours shut in that study, the furtive phone calls, his worries about money. He was in on it. He had betrayed her. That was why he was so keen for her to abandon her fight against the state, *that* was why he called her crazy, *that* was why he said she'd been putting the twins at risk – at risk from his hideous plans for them. How long had he been part of it? Her heart raced. Since his move into the vagaries of 'IT'. How could she have missed that? The perverted activities hidden in plain sight. IT. Infant trafficking!

Margot launched herself out of bed, barrelling into the en suite and vomiting her guts into the toilet bowl.

For the next couple of days, she stonewalled the sick bastard as she worked out what to do. There was really only one option. The people he'd called to take their children could already be on their way. She had to protect the boys, or risk losing them forever.

The day is coming.

The day was coming. It was almost here. November 5th. Set by Bert Colbert, the Day of Frenzy, when the people would rise and the truth would be revealed. The anniversary of the historic attempt to overthrow the deep state, which had sadly failed, and the date chosen by this corrupt government to flex its authoritarian muscles by implementing yet another illegal lockdown.

This is your day. This is your time to act.

Margot knew what she had to do; she knew it was right, her only option, but that didn't make it any easier. As she settled down to sleep on the night of the fourth, she felt nauseous to the pit of her stomach. She'd been getting breathless all day, which she put down to the nerves and adrenaline of what was to come. She'd kissed Miles and Giles goodnight, before glaring with distaste at the man still lying recumbent in a sweaty heap in their bed. 'You'll pay,' she whispered. 'All of you will pay.'

At 5AM, Margot was standing in the kitchen, silver moonlight falling on her skin as she gazed out the window. She didn't see the autumn darkness, she saw her children laughing and playing in the sunshine throughout their seven precious years. Margot grabbed what she needed, and returned to her bedroom.

Derek had done little but sleep since he'd started feigning his 'illness' to throw her off the scent of what he was really up to. He was sleeping now, a throttled snore whining through his nostrils, as Margot padded across the soft rug, stepped up onto their king-size bed, and climbed on top of him. Then he woke.

'Margot. Why – why are you wet? You're soaking,' he said, dazed.

She ignored him, reaching over to unplug his bedside lamp and replace it with what she'd brought from the kitchen.

'What's going on?' Derek coughed, a sound like splintered wood on granite.

'Doing what I have to do,' Margot muttered. 'Doing what you evil bastards forced me to.'

Derek's tired eyes were adjusting to the darkness. He squinted, trying to make out what his wife was holding up as though she were going to stake him like a vampire. 'Is that the bl—'

The rest of the word was shoved back down his windpipe as Margot brought the blender down to dock onto his Adam's apple. Bitter tears budded as her fists squeezed the button.

Whrzzzz! The blades stuttered on sweaty skin. Derek gasped, tried to cry out. Margot pressed harder. *Whrrrchhhh.* The motor ground for all its top-of-the-range might. As Derek grabbed her thighs, Margot shifted, giving her the tilt she needed. The blender found purchase, sinking its steel teeth into flesh, sawing hungrily into cartilage.

Now Derek screamed.

Whrizzz!

Ribbons of blood lashed her cheeks, redecorating their bedroom in seconds. Her husband's hands slamming against her legs, nails clawing at her stomach, Margot held firm, pushing at his neck as though with an angle grinder. Derek bucked, spewing gore across the sheets. The blender became a piston, ploughing in and out of the hollow beneath his chin. Blood welled out in gallons like newly discovered oil. *Whrrrtttt.* The blades stuttered as they chewed through tongue, severing it and his screams as one.

And then he was still. Eyes an endless stare to the heavens. Throat collapsed into a pit of rustic salsa. Margot tossed the blender aside and dismounted with a shuddering, angry breath.

You are a warrior. A saviour.

Margot grabbed her car keys and left the house. Her *Covid-1984* pyjamas, soaked in crimson, flapped against her bare ankles. Gripped by an iron focus, she strode across the lawn, lit by the first rosy hint of dawn. She walked past the climbing frame, the curvaceous flower beds, the badminton net, the pool where her boys floated facedown among the autumn leaves. She saw none of it.

Opening up the garage, Margot jumped into her Toyota, revved up the self-charging hybrid engine and placed her phone on the dashboard, flipping the camera to selfie mode and hitting record.

'This is the day. Our day. The day we free the truth and the world wakes up to everything they're doing to us.'

Foot on the accelerator.

Let's go.

Red rage thundered in her temples as she tore out of the village, towards town. Her forehead was searing, like someone was pressing a hot brand into her skull. Everywhere, outside, sheeple in their face-nappies. Margot wanted to roll down the window and screech at them, *Don't you see what you're walking into? Don't you know what they're doing?*

A crusty cough burbled out of her throat and the Toyota swerved out of lane, earning angry honks from other motorists.

Concentrate.

Margot tried. Her nerves were frayed, sick sweat running in rivulets down her torso. She had the wheel in a death-grip (the same death-grip that had, a short time before, held the heads of Miles and Giles underwater even as they bawled and thrashed).

'Here it is,' she said to her phone, still recording, as St Jude's came into view. 'I'll show you what they don't want you to see. I'll show you the empty hospital. Expose their Convid-19. Topple their pack of lies. The only thing in that building is hundreds of innocent children tortured in the name of their scientific experiments.'

Speaking her truth brought the months of revelations she'd experienced flooding through her mind again all at once. The decimation of livelihoods and lives, of freedom, good business, mental health, education, the lies, the fear, manipulation and oppression, the perversion and corruption. It made her furious.

The mighty hospital filled her windscreen. A nurse, wheeling an elderly man in through the doors, both of them masked up.

'He's not sick!' she screeched. 'There's nothing wrong with him, except you lot smothering his airways!'

Perhaps they couldn't hear, or were ignoring her, so Margot ploughed her palm into the horn. The nurse turned, frowned, and carried on walking.

Something snapped. Bare toes curled on the pedal. Muscles tensed, teeth ground. Margot *roared*. The Toyota slammed forward. Tarmac skidded away beneath its wheels. St Jude's entrance ballooned towards her. Parking sensors screamed. And for one brief, fragile moment, Margot was flying, in perfect serenity, enlightened, in true frenzy.

Glass doors cascaded over the bonnet, metal frames twisted in architectural agony. Staff leaped and scrambled in fear. Alarms wailed. Her phone sailed from the dashboard. Margot juddered forward, the cushion of the airbag pouncing from the steering wheel to smack her into oblivion.

Beep. Beep. Beep.

The beeping is a lullaby compared to the clattering, rattling, slapping of shoes on tiles. The coughing, the spluttering, the sobbing. You wake to white light, clinical light, turquoise curtains and blue-aproned figures.

Doctors, wrapped up like hazardous waste, faces obscured behind perspex visors, fuss around you, checking you, machines, drips.

You try to shout. Your throat is raw, your tongue sandpaper. Molten sweat rolls off your brow.

You want to scream at them, berate them for their part in the hostile takeover of society. Tell them the disease is a hoax. Tell them everyone is well. The hospitals are empty. These people? They're crisis actors. Look! That man over there, being given the oxygen, you've seen him on Line of Duty. *The 'doctors' and 'nurses' – they're the very same thespians forced out of work by our corrupt lawmakers!*

They look at you with pity and pain. Perhaps they know what you've done. But you had no choice. You did what any rational mother would do. You had to protect your boys. You had to protect them from their father's despicable plan, from the people coming to take them. And in any case, what Orwellian future would they have faced otherwise?

You see the TV in the corner. Reporting on what you've done. What you've done. You, singular. Where is the Day of Frenzy? Where is the uprising? Bert Colbert issuing a statement, condemning the actions of a 'lone nutter who does not represent our peaceful campaign for freedom'. Mums Against Masks has disbanded, its admins admonishing themselves of any association with Margot Kyle.

Suddenly you feel very alone.

You look to your left, seeking some human connection. The man in that bed is glaring at you. It takes you a moment to recognise him beneath the oxygen mask strapped across his face. Kickbox! No, what's his actual name... Darren?

You try to explain, to tell him that what you were doing was right, that it is everyone else who is blind to reality. He closes his eyes and turns away.

Then you realise why he won't listen. He can't hear you, can't understand your words. A blue blur across your nose, stale breath brushing your lips. They've muzzled you! You lift a hand to try and tear the mask away, but your wrist is caught. The other, too. You're cuffed to the bed frame.

Police officers approach you.

Panic rises like a geyser. The bed shudders. You writhe and struggle but it's helpless. They've got you trapped.

'Get away!' you scream. 'I know what you are. I know all about the deep state and you will not take me.'

This one has heard you.

He leans in close, and in the eyes above his mask, you see nothing but darkness. 'Ma'am,' he says, 'the only deep state here is the one we've found you in today.'

BURN

You watch through the window as we die. We're clawing at the glass, framed like an exhibit. Silenced, on your side. For a moment I think your expression is impassive, then I realise it's seeped with bitterness and grit. You're forcing yourself to stay and witness my family's demise.

ZACH

2055.

I skim through my tab as we glide through city streets. Today the smog is wildfire orange outside Darren's car – the Mercedes gifted by his father. It presses against the windscreen, cloaking everything in our path; people leer out from it like ghouls. Inside we're cool, swept by the icy breeze from the car's inbuilt Airway.

I swipe away articles on the latest rats caught crossing from North Africa, India and even further afield. Over ten thousand washed up already this summer, they say. God knows why they'd want to come here. Our Augusts are pushing forty-five degrees. It's hard to breathe outside, let alone walk more than a few metres without the sun stripping the sweat from your scalp. We see them now, outside the car. People collapsing in the street.

'Slow down,' Mikey says, rolling open his window. He launches a handful of ice cubes into the crowd. One hits a lady on the temple. She stops, confused, dropping her shopping bag. Most of them seem dazed – heat zombies. Some scrabble for the ice, hold it to their chests like holy relics. The boys laugh. I'm filming it on my tab.

We move on. I share the footage on Bubble, along with hundreds of other pranks we've done. The views on one from last week are rocketing. We made ice cream in my mum's machine to give out for free in town. People love free ice cream, until they realise it's laced with Tabasco.

We get out of the car to stretch our legs. The heat is stifling; it presses in at us from all directions. We have handheld Airways, sucking through the fetid air, filtering and cooling it into refreshing blades. Streetfolk regard us with resentment. I know they think we're arrogant rich kids – but why should we suffer just because we can afford not to?

'Excuse me? Excuse me, buddy?' A man – middle aged – stooped. He's looking directly at me with what takes me a moment to realise is deference. I feel a connection strike up against my will.

'Yeah?' I say.

'Can I have a quick go on that?' he asks, indicating my Airway. 'Do you mind?'

Mikey steps in, all toothy grin. 'Here, use mine.' As he hands the man his Airway, he slips me a smirk and whispers, 'Film this, Zach.'

I tap the button on my tab, hold it recording by my hip. The man is thanking us, fumbling with the unfamiliar device, beads of embarrassment mingling with the heat sweats running down his neck. He dials it on. The mouth of the Airway glows red. He has no idea Mikey has switched the function, until a roasting blast sears the anticipation right off his face.

He stumbles back, gasping, skin blotchy and flaring, unable to talk. Darren sniggers. Mikey grabs the Airway off him. 'Sorry, mate, you must've flipped it onto heat mode,' he says, struggling to keep a straight face.

I feel bad, and chuck him a bottle of Evian SelfCool from my bag as we leave. It bounces off his feet, where he's collapsed on the pavement. Before I turn away, a woman runs to help him. He locks eyes with me again and that deference has turned to naked hurt.

•

We live in a private compound just outside the city. Anyone with a bit of money has had to fortify their property. It's a walled oasis, all anthracite metal beams, plate glass walls and irrigated lawns. I slip my shoes off and pad over cool granite tiles to flop on the sofa. The room – like the rest of our house – is chilled by Airways mounted on every ceiling.

I see Mum on her sunbed out in the garden by the pool. Earbuds in, listening to some godawful old popstar, no doubt. We even have Airways outside, pumping out deliciously refrigerated air so we can relax beside the pool in comfort year-round.

Alone in the house, bored, I watch old videos of Dad on TV. He's saved them in a playlist.

'At the heart of this issue is freedom. Personal liberty. The freedoms that have been long fought for and hard won. Our society is built on freedom. These eco-zealots want to take that away from us. You should be free to choose where your energy comes from, what kind of car you drive, how often you go on holiday, what food you eat. I say enough is enough. If we're going to survive, we must do so in a world worth living in. A free world.'

It's from the mid-twenties, some debate show. He's handsome, strong, charismatic. The people he's arguing with don't stand a chance; he can talk over them with the might of a tank and the eloquence of a preacher.

'We have to be reasonable here. Even if the so-called "science" – which, by the way, no one agrees upon – is true, we shouldn't have to sacrifice our present to prevent some unproven trouble in the future. Humans adapt. That's how we dominated this planet. We simply cannot allow elitist bureaucrats to pour eye-watering sums of our money into this "net zero" guff, especially when their draconian policies will hurt the poorest of us hardest, all the while China is laughing and polluting as we wreck our economy to make diddly-squat of an impact. Trust me, there is no need to panic.'

It's electric. Dick Talbot, my father, catches a note in the public mood and spins it into a symphony. He becomes the face of the climate critical movement. Threatened industries pay him handsomely to speak on TV, radio, social media and front ghost-written articles and books. Free market individualism is defended, and I'm born into a world where we can choose how we want to live out our lives.

He's my fucking hero.

Nowadays he only needs to make the occasional public appearance. He was rewarded handsomely for his hard work, and grows those rewards through canny investments, always driving for more. He never stops networking, so most of the time it's just me and Mum (a successful culinary influencer in her own right) at home.

Until you arrive.

LARA

You've never known hunger. Not the kind that gnaws through your stomach and saps your brainpower. Not the kind you have to take to bed, before it greets you with a bite in the morning. Not the kind my people know, Zach.

But even your caste has begun to feel the – if not collapse – then tremors in your food supply. Price hikes, empty shelves, ugly produce, no matter how far you pay to get things shipped. I hear some of you are shelling out to have hydroponic units installed in your properties, fostering a reliable crop to your programmed demands, under sterile lights, calibrated temperatures and automated irrigation.

I observe your family from a distance for months, following, discovering. I see the pictures your mother posts of the meals she makes, or orders. I see the videos you share of the locals you humiliate, or torture. I see your father's appearances on the news blaming the cesspit this country's become on the 'hoards of migrants flooding our borders'. He never calls us rats, at least not publicly. In private, I'm not so sure.

Then I see you up close. I'm watching as you play that cruel trick on the man with your handheld heater. I run to him as you walk away, hold his hand as he pants on the pavement, anoint his head with the water you discarded.

In that moment I hate you. Before, in my eyes, you'd just been a child. An offshoot of a soulless father and vapid mother. But now I know the insidiousness of your clan, I realise you deserve everything my people have planned.

•

An eighteen-wheeler comes over on the ferry from Calais. It docks in Dover, but doesn't make it a mile before coming to a halt. The port is gridlocked, lorries packed in like bricks. It's the hottest day of the year – so far. A record in Kent. Some of the vehicles were stopped by customs, others by the melting road surface. The gridlock lasts three days. The driver has to abandon his truck and sleep in the lobby of a nearby hotel.

When the dock finally clears, the driver returns to his vehicle, moving it on to the checkpoint. The man there to take it over is pissed at the delay. He grabs the keys, hauls himself up behind the wheel and sets off. He never asks what he's delivering – that's not his job. But this time he can smell it.

He steers the truck into a layby. Then he switches off the engine and walks away into the woods. He never checks his cargo.

It's not discovered until the following week, after the heatwave has been broken by thunderous downpour. Ramblers report it to police. Police uncover the bodies. Twenty-nine humans – men, women and infants. The stench makes the officers retch. They find fingers raw from prising at the truck doors, throats parched as desert rock, skin a papery crust. Flies growing fat on boiled flesh.

You may think of those bodies as rats. But six of them were my family.

•

You answer the door to me. Maybe there's a hint of recognition, a face glimpsed on the crowded street.

'There's a problem with your Hydropod connection,' I say. 'I've come to fix it.'

Your eyes flick down to my breasts before you shrug and let me in. Then you wander off to your teenage pursuits, playing video games, masturbating or plotting more ways to humiliate the desperate.

My feet pace across the granite tiles, as I gaze in awe at this domestic cathedral. I can't help myself. I'm jealous. Your rooms are more like those of an art gallery than a dwelling – spacious, minimal, glistening with the sheen of money. I pass through the living room and into the kitchen.

'Who are you?'

I'm startled. I thought we were alone in the house.

The woman approaches me with suspicion. Your mother – Jules.

'My name's Lara,' I say. 'I've been sent to fix your Hydropod.'

She frowns. 'I didn't think there was anything wrong with it.'

'Yes,' I reply. 'It's working fine for you?'

'It is.'

'That's great. Then the issue is just the network connection. For our remote monitoring, you see. Fault detection, over-the-air updates, that kind of thing.'

I wait. Her flawless features are unreadable. A bead of sweat rolls down my spine, despite your precision-cooled kitchen. She nods. 'OK, it's this way.'

Jules leads me through to the pantry where the hydroponic unit is housed. Clearly uninterested in bestowing any more of her time on me, she drifts off. But before she goes, I ask her to share the property's network details. She obliges, making my job a whole lot easier. I tap them into my tab. I'm in, and ready to play my role in the action we've been planning for months.

I climb into the moulded white booth, a cavern of light and vertical planting. The door sealed, I'm safe in the calibrated environment, independent from the rest of the house. You'll forget that I'm here. I'll wait till the sun sets, and your daddy comes home. Then it's time to make you pay.

ZACH

I wake from stifling dreams to crushing heat. In the darkness I fling off the covers, a dead weight. Flip the pillow, roll over, but it's no good – my head is radiating like a furnace. Something's wrong. We've had hot nights before, but nothing like this. It shouldn't be like this in our house.

I go over to my windows. They're shut. Wave my hand by the sensor. Nothing. 'Windows, open,' I say. Nothing.

The air is pressing close against me. Sweat glues my t-shirt to my back. I stagger out from my bedroom. Mum is on the landing, red-faced, faint. I try to call out to her, but her grip on the bannister fails. She collapses down the staircase.

My own hands are shaking. They're red too. Everything is red. Hot air gusts against my neck and I look up. The mouth of the Airway mounted on the ceiling is glowing.

'Fuck.' Dad, he's seen it too. His feet thump across the landing, down the stairs. His vest is soaked through.

I go after him. My knees give way. The air is a little cooler at the floor, through my hands on the tiles. I gulp it in like a landed fish. I see Dad clamber over the heap of Mum's body at the bottom of the stairs. I follow.

He's bashing the home's control screen, muttering and swearing. On the ground floor, every Airway I see is pulsing red. 'What's happened?' I ask. The words wrench my throat as if they were lodged bones.

He ignores me, tapping at his tab now. 'Nothing getting through…'

Every movement makes my skin slick, sweat-sodden pyjamas weighing me down. Each gulp of breath is hotter than the last. I'm reduced to a panting dog.

Dad strides to the front door. Locked. He presses his fingerprint against the sensor. Still locked. Tries the voice command. Nothing. He kicks it and swears as toes meet armoured steel.

I haul myself into the kitchen. Flop against the sink. Turn on the tap ready for the merciful flow. Steaming water scolds my face. 'Shit!' I cry. 'Cold! Cold!' The tap doesn't respond. I slide down the cabinet, sobbing.

Crawling across the floor – the only movement I can manage now is crawling – I see Dad trying the patio doors, the windows, anything, but nothing. He launches a chair at the glass, but it bounces off, useless. Reinforced. Now he's staggering like a boar shot with a dart gun. Gasping and panting, he flings open the bathroom door. 'Fuck!' he yells as he finds the taps in there set to boiling temperatures too. Then I see him squat over the toilet bowl, sloshing his face with palmfuls of its contents.

How has our house turned against us? Why?

I claw my way back to the kitchen, my vision beginning to blur and sway. I grasp the metal legs of a stool at the breakfast bar, attempt to hurl it at the crimson gape of the Airway above. It barely leaves my grip, clattering across the floor. I join it.

And as I rest my searing cheek against the tiles, I see you creeping out of your hidey hole.

LARA

I can't resist. I have to see how this ends. Tearing some leafy stems from the nearest plant, I dip them in the water trough and wrap them round my head to keep me cool. Then I leave the Hydropod, stepping out into the furnace your home has become, and locking the unit behind me.

I see you on the kitchen floor, a prone curl, like a fleck of snot or a beach worm. You look more like a child than how I've come to perceive you. My breath rasps hot against my mask of leaves. I can't stay here long.

Your eye rolls up as I approach. There's no surprise or sorrow in it, only rage. 'Wh... why?' you croak.

Perhaps you think I'm an eco-terrorist, here to punish you for your lives of high consumption and casual destruction. A radical idealist who believes taking out those at the top will spill their spoils to those down below. A jealous anti-capitalist on a mission to blow up everything your society has built.

You would be wrong. I am every one of those things, and more.

Your daddy didn't just get rich from acting the corporate shill for the crumbling titans of pollution. He partnered with the money men. He made the investments. As he championed the freedom to choose, the freedom to pollute, the freedom to cook our world alive, he helped seed the industries that would rise up to feed on its carcass. He could pick his winners - Airways, Hydropods… and illicit transportation. Once whole continents became inhospitable, the men he funded were there waiting to smuggle desperate populations across ever more hostile borders. They called us rats fleeing sinking ships, but the captains of the ships that picked us up got rich indeed. Your father continued to spread lies and sow division, making the crossings ever more treacherous – and expensive. Many never reached their destination. They died like my relatives, poisoned by heat in the back of abandoned lorries, but their drivers still pocketed the cash. Cash that trickled back upstream into your deep pockets. Cash to be gorged on, or gambled on the weather markets, or ploughed into weaponry start-ups, booming from the social unrest.

'You see, Zach,' I say. 'Families like yours have been in the driving seat for far too long. If this world is going to survive, we're going to have to take that wheel by force.'

With that I leave you. You crawl, huffing and puffing, behind me. Jules and Dick join you, in a delirious scramble to catch me. But you're all far too weak. I'm out the door, unlocked by my tab just for me, and out onto your Airway-chilled patio. You hammer on the glass of your grand front room window, choking, sweating, bleeding. I back away, dipping my feet in your pool, feeling cold at the sight of this grotesque family portrait, framed just for me.

CUTTER

Cutting isn't an addiction. I'm not chasing that first high like a desperate loser. If anything, it gets better. And before you get the wrong idea, I'm not talking about the pity-whoring teens slicing up their wrists in biology class type of cutting – I'm talking get out the chainsaw and make some fucking woodchips cutting.

Trees. I'm cutting trees.

I go out under cover of darkness, when you're all tucked up in bed, safe from the beggars and the rapers prowling the streets. In a good night, I can hit seven or eight. I could do more – obviously – but I like to savour the fun for all involved.

Clusters are my signature. A nice avenue, or a cul de sac. The residents go beddy-byes, all at peace in their fragile lives, then wake to find their darling promenade of cherry trees slain. Trunks severed, stumps all asplinter, blossom-spewing branches heaped on the pavement.

Mrs Jenkins at Number 3 is the first to discover the crime, throwing back her curtains to unveil the massacre. She yelps. Does a double take. Calls her husband Bernard over to verify the horror. Before she's even dressed, she's texting Margaret across the street and soon every neighbour is out their front door. Ba-da-boom, we have a street party!

Gasps of disbelief ('Who would do such a thing?'), consoling hugs, more than a few tears – Eleanor's girl is even on the ground clasping a severed cherry branch to her breast.

Oh, it's a giggle. And we're just getting started.

•

I don't witness this melodramatic scene first-hand, of course. By daybreak, I am gone. No hanging around to soak up the teary aftermath. I'm not a psycho.

My favourite ones to fell are the sprouters of around five years. Those just about ready to outgrow their stabilising stakes and ties. When the trunk is somewhere between the thickness of an anorexic's arm and a heffer's thigh. An age at which the neighbourhood watchers assume the sapling is out of the woods, so to speak, and heading for maturity.

It takes my blade less than thirty seconds to chew through each trunk.

Years of life, pruning, tending, watering, budding and blossoming. *Brzzz. Chrzzkk*. Timber! And *fin*.

I started with flowers. Spring nights out with Gran's secateurs. Creeping along cottage gardens as the daffodils bloomed. Chop chop chop – off with their heads.

But it's not quite enough with those piddly plants. They grow back too fast, and their severed lifespan isn't substantial enough to merit much mourning. Also, you have to cut a hell of a lot of them to make an impact. No, trees are the real deal. And once I got my hands on Granddad's old chainsaw, they were at my mercy.

At first, the odd arboreal casualty was deemed an accident. A vehicle swerving across the kerb. Delinquent youths blowing off steam with their mates. But when the numbers started racking up, the *Enquirer* deemed it a 'spate'. My first press coverage. And once it was in print, the world (well, the local ward) took note.

I found the group on Facebook. It was open, so I joined. *Catch the Ladbrook Grove Tree Killer*, founded by Tracey Beale. Oh Tracey, you crack me up. The title was just the tip of the exciteberg. The hysterical comments were, well, hysterical:

How could someone be so evil?!

Have you seen the acer by the Eddington Road post office? The owner (nice Indian man) was devastated.

This is NOT what we need in a #ClimateEmergency!

Who eva did this should be shot – or locked up!!

I like and comment along with the rest of them. (*B*stards who do dis shd be sawed in harf!*) I get a lot of thumbs up. Or rather, Chip Wood and his hunky stock-image avatar do.

Discussion is thriving. Theories, psychoanalyses and fears abound. It's the hallmark of gang warfare. A series of copycats. A disgruntled ex-park ranger.

I despair for humanity. This is why we can't have nice things.

It's an expression of sexual impotence. An act of eco futility in the face of global annihilation. Video game violence made flesh.

We have 2 protect are treees!

Speculation: where might he strike next? Ladbrook Grove Community Centre? The Promenade? Deenside Wildlife Reserve?!

All good ideas, thank you very much.

•

The fact is I don't have an agenda. I'm not trying to impart some grand, important message. If anything, it's the opposite. By chopping down a street tree, I'm merely demonstrating how pointless it was. How swiftly it can be rendered obsolete. When the council whines about how each felling costs it upwards of £100 to clear away (seriously), or the local community wails and tears at their clothes, my point – if there is one – is proven. You think a poxy sycamore will soak up all the pollution your SUV lifestyle pumps into the atmosphere? You think your road should be garlanded with cherry blossom, while the estate round the corner is sprinkled with soiled needles and condoms? You think sticking a plaque on a horse chestnut is gonna be appreciated by your dead relative?

Jesus, give me a break.

•

Do these people not realise how public their group is? I hope not, because it's proving a great resource. I catch neighbours hatching plans to police their streets, coordinating lookouts to keep their cherished trees safe from Lumberjack the Ripper.

I pick Holly and Joe's watch. They're guarding a lovely newbuild development, set on the flattened remains of what was once a heap of benefits. At midnight, I pull up just round the corner, cranking the handbrake of my Astra. I lean forwards to scan the street.

It's quiet. Parked cars and young staked poplars flanking both sides of the road. And right on cue, there's Holly, coddled in her fluffy dressing gown, poking her head out the front door – the regular check-up throughout her promised hours of surveillance.

I take my chainsaw (a nimble, battery powered baby much more suited to these jobs than Grandpa's) and slip from the car. I creep along the pavement across the road from Holly's terrace, all-black attire swallowed by the shadows. Crouching behind a Range Rover, I wait.

Not all the surrounding shithole estates have yet been flushed, so it's not long before a boy racer comes screeching down the tarmac, straight from shifting some smack, or smacking some bitch. And that's my cue.

Hit the button. Saw buzzes into life. Slip it between the stakes. Quick slice across the slender trunk. Time of death: 12.06.

The severed canopy slumps forward, caught by the rubber tie still holding it to the stakes. If Holly peeps out now, she probably won't even notice a thing.

I move onto the next tree, await a passing motor and *brzzz*. Another one down.

Now three's where things get dicey. It starts well – I cut through just as a backfiring car trundles past. But the blade catches on a splinter as I tug it free. The top half of the trunk slips from the bottom, shooting down like a battering ram into the side of a stationary BMW. A beat to suck in breath, before the alarm squeals into ear-splitting, head-crashing life.

I dart back down the street, crouched low to the ground. Holly – or someone – howls, perhaps spotting the malformed slouch of the poplar in the BMW's flashing spotlight.

Breath ragged, I make it back to my car, fling the chainsaw onto the passenger seat and floor it out of there. I curse myself all the way home. What good is half – or even just a third – of a road felled?

•

The war escalates.

We have to be more vigilant! screamed Sharon on the Facebook group. *This evil monster is getting away with it right under our noses!*

Discussion rages, and I lap it up.

Then a bomb goes off.

Surprisingly, the tree that does it is not, to me, one of my most notable works. An inauspicious rowan in Sam Hill Park that I slew on a whim on my way back from a hit on a nearby nursery. Turns out there was some tit nest up in the branches and so – a few cracked egg pics later – the Facebook group is *incensed*.

He must be targeting the ones that will cause the most hurt to our community. We can't protect every tree but we MUST protect the most special ones.

There follows a thread, poll and another thread to decide, exactly, which are those most special trees to this most special community.

I copy down the list, swapping the numbers for checkboxes.

First up: Ellen Wren's memorial magnolia.

•

Wind shrieks through the streets as I go to guard Ellen's tree. I zip my coat up tight and pull down the hood. At the entrance to Ladbrook Grove Community Garden, I see my partner for the night – an old man holding an LED camping lantern.

'Stephen,' he introduces himself.

'Chip,' I say, shaking his wrinkly hand.

Catch the Ladbrook Grove Tree Killer has over a hundred members now, all on high alert. The affront to their earnest sensibilities has gone on too long. The 'extremely vulnerable' list has round the clock protection. So of course, Chip Wood was happy to volunteer his time.

'Old picture,' I explain, in case the decrepit geezer is wondering why I don't match the airbrushed cheekbones of my online persona, but I suspect he can't discern much through his mildewed corneas anyway.

Stephen and I shuffle into the parklet, receiving a hallowed nod from Holly and Joe (pretty sure they're having an affair) as we take over the watch.

Ellen's tree is a substantial – and very pretty – magnolia, just coming into flower. I peruse the memorial plaque, though I've already ingested her story online. She was a sweet girl at the secondary school across the road when she dropped down dead in the woods on her way home – asthma attack. Twenty years later and bingo, she's outlived her mortal years as some kind of symbol of virtuous innocence the locals can pay homage to when they take out their pooch for a crap. You know the council rinses you for a grand to name a tree in your dearly decaying's memory – *a fucking grand*?! And that's just for a ten-year contract. You wanna stop them slapping some other dead fucker's name on it a decade in, you gotta renew your fucking subscription.

Stephen's brought a foldout camping stool along with his lantern. He plonks it down and settles his creaking bones atop it. I have something very different in my rucksack.

He bitches on in his raspy old man whine about how dreadful it is that someone could carry out this 'monstrous reign of vandalism' in Ladbrook, but how it has 'warmed his heart' than the community has rallied round to protect its 'shared heritage'. Pass me the bucket.

I nod and mumble 'absolutely's, all the while masking my bemusement with these people. Or maybe it's amusement. Do you not see how ludicrous it is to believe you have any more right to a neighbourhood filled with leafy branches, than I have a right to chop them down? You have no rights at all. Trees have no more right to grow than little Ellen did when she took her last gasp under their canopy. Your rules and codes, taboos and morals are entirely artificial. I opted out of them a long time ago.

'– and we're thinking of holding a vigil for the trees we've lost,' Stephen is saying, 'silent, candle lit –'

'Coffee?' I offer, interrupting his tiresome spiel.

'Oh. OK, thank you.'

I pour him a cup from my Thermos, a delicious concoction of Columbian roast and Superdrug laxatives. With the darkness and his cataracts, he doesn't notice me emptying my cup out on the grass.

'Mm,' he says on the first sip. 'Urhm,' he says ten minutes later, a hand on his burbling belly. And soon, as cold sweat beads, 'Oh god…'

'There's some bushes in the far corner,' I say.

The old man clutches his gut, his expression a delightful highspeed montage of dread, horror, anguish and acceptance. He dashes off into the undergrowth.

And that's my cue. Trusty chainsaw out the bag, revved up and sunk into Ellen's tree. The magnolia's sturdier than my usual victims and it takes a bit of pressure to get the battery saw to bite. But it doesn't let me down. Teeth chew into bark. Splinters fly like confetti. I grin like a simpleton.

'Nooo!' Stephen roars, racing out of the hedge in a limping old man gait, one hand holding up his khakis by the belt buckle. He's surprisingly fast. 'You bastard!' He reaches out to stop me, lunging at speed. I meet him with a side kick to the stomach. 'Oof', he says, tumbling to the ground with the squit of voiding bowels.

Back to my task. I tug the chainsaw free in a shriek of shattered wood. Then all it takes is a final shove and the magnolia topples, trunk snapping, budding branches slapping the ground. I think Stephen is actually crying.

•

I stroll back through the night, whistling gaily in the roaring wind. I cut through the park, the scene of many of my exploratory crimes. My golden age is just beginning, I think, as I potter down the avenue of old oaks.

Something catches my ear. A faint squeak beyond the gales. High pitched, like a mewling kitten. I pause, and look up. No cat. Then I barely have time to think '*And when the bough breaks...*' before, well, the bough breaks.

With an almighty crack, it falls.

Moonlight twinkles through the leaves. Life flashes before my eyes. Childhood treats. Ice cream. Donkey rides. Cycling without stabilisers, through this very park. Gran, Granddad, aunts and uncles. Friends, enemies, teachers, counsellors. School halls, movie theatres, church halls,

A&Es. Pizza brekkies, coke nights, stealing ciggies, festival toilets, silent deathbeds, angry hook-ups, ruining weddings, pavement head-cracks, kicking toddlers, one more tinny –

I step to the side, and the branch crashes at my feet.

I give it a disinterested nudge with my trainer. You didn't think it was going to crush me, did you? Nature's revenge for slaughtering her offspring? A lump of wood turning your boy into a puddle of pulp on the ground? Come on, you know that's not how it works. There's no divine justice here, or anywhere.

We all just fuck around, doing whatever the fuck we want to each other, and the more awful we behave, the fewer the consequences.

You precious fucking idiot.

THE KING IS DEAD, PART III

De Luz, California. 8th August 2019.

Trees whipped past the window: pine, conifer, redwood. Sun bled through the branches, its warmth intangible beyond the confines of their air-conditioned vehicle. Andrea shifted in her seat, clothes scratching on leather, trying to stretch out her aching shoulders. Reflected in the glass, she could see Xand in the seat beside her, skimming through emails on his laptop. Occasionally he'd break the silence to ask his assistant in the front to schedule a call or follow up on some report, and she would jot the task down in her phone.

About half an hour from the nearest town, they turned off into the woods. A mile or so of dirt track and they passed under a wrought iron archway in a high wall, gates opening at their approach, flanked by security cameras. The metal above them was woven into intricate lettering: *CASTLE COOL*. It felt so out of place in the sun-drenched

Californian woodland that it gave Andrea a shudder, as though she were in the opening act of a horror movie.

Leaning forward, she peered through the windscreen. 'We're here,' she muttered. Xand only spared the view a momentary glance from hammering on his keyboard. Their driver pulled into a parking area, wheels crunching on gravel, attracting the attention of the only other soul in the woods. The pantsuited lady gave a start, before trotting over from her Tesla, teeth gleaming like a row of foglights beneath cropped bleach blonde hair.

Andrea had barely got out of the car before the woman thrust a hand towards her. 'Harriet Collins,' she said, clipboard pinned under an arm. 'Realtor.'

'Andrea,' she replied. 'Writer. I'm with Xand Goetz.' *Thankfully not for much longer*, she added in her head.

Xand sloped out of the vehicle, passing his laptop to his assistant without a word and giving Harriet a disinterested nod. He put on a pair of sunglasses from the pocket of his sharp Armani shirt, and frowned up at the building.

'So this is it,' he said.

'This is it,' Harriet echoed, with a heavy injection of cheer. 'And what a property – a marvel – it is.'

That it was. A full-scale medieval stone castle, each corner of its battlements pinned by a pointed tower at least five stories high, surrounded by a twenty-foot moat. Andrea had known what to expect, at least on paper, but the sheer scale of the place was overwhelming. *So it's real*, she thought, but every step towards the Castle felt like she was stepping further into a dream.

'Before we come to the main residence, you will of course be aware that the property also includes fourteen-hundred acres of surrounding land,' Harriet was saying. 'Trees, mostly. All walled in, with total security monitoring for peace of mind. On the left you have the hedge maze, rather overgrown at present.' She indicated the leafy bushes stretching away at an angle beside them. Harriet knew that the maze formed the outline of a diamond from above. 'But you could of course have that removed and use the space for, say, a tennis court or guest house.'

'I thought there already was a tennis court?' Xand interjected.

'Yes, of course, yes there is.' Harriet seemed flustered, in a bright, perky way. 'Beyond the Castle, there are a couple of courts, that's right. And on our other side are the stables and paddocks. Empty now, of course.'

A stone bridge crossed the moat to the entrance of the Castle. Andrea peered over the edge, but only a trail of thick sludge remained between the dried-out banks. Topping that up must have sucked this parched state dry.

'The moat is pumped from the local reservoir,' Harriet said, spotting her interest. 'It has, of course, been turned off for a few years now, but at the push of a button you'll have this filled to the brim with the finest water in California. So clean you could drink it!'

Andrea nodded, not trusting herself to speak. At the entrance – a grand archway carved into the wall with towering oak doors – she traced a hand over the stone front of the building. 'It's real,' she whispered.

Xand frowned at her.

'I just... I don't know,' Andrea said. 'I kind of expected it to be like a movie set or something, made of polystyrene.'

'Everything about this place is real,' Harriet said. 'That was the spirit of the Castle, through and through.' She stopped, as if realising she might have said something inappropriate, but relaxed when it didn't trigger any reaction from her viewers.

Harriet opened the doors and the trio entered the home of the late Dante DaSilva. Having seen the extensive brochure, Andrea knew what to expect in the grandeur of Castle Cool – or, as the property was being marketed, the Faversham Estate. That was its original name before DaSilva bought it from the family of the newspaper magnate in the early nineties, hot on the success of his third platinum studio album, *The King of Cool*. A coronated millionaire needed a castle. He expanded and renovated the existing mansion, creating the mock medieval palace he would live in until his heart attack in 2007. Since then the building had remained empty, with no takers for the $500 million price tag that DaSilva's estate desired. Over the years the price was cut: $300, $250, $100, $75 million... Then when the explosive revelations about the pop icon's history of abuse blasted his legacy to shrapnel, the Castle was cursed. No one could see anything but the repulsive activities inflicted on so many children within these walls, described so explicitly in the documentaries, articles and books by his victims. And yet, two years later, here was Alexander Goetz, chequebook in hand.

Why would he want to buy this place? Andrea studied him as they toured the building, trying to discern anything in the chiselled face that would accompany her profile in *Silicon Valley Insider*. Her editor had already sent her the header: *The Man Who Changed the Way We Pay.* Though she'd spent a week shadowing the eponymous man for her story, she felt no closer to an answer.

Harriet led them through vast kitchens, dining halls, guest rooms, music studio, and a home cinema bigger than many independent picture houses Andrea had visited. The rooms connected the Castle's corner towers, with a courtyard in the centre. She looked out on the paved space through diamond-shaped windows. They reminded her of her tip – *Look behind the gold diamond.* That was what the maid had said. While the agent regaled them with the property's history (omitting notable chunks) and features, Andrea's eyes roved across the rooms, searching for any sign of a gold diamond.

The house had been gutted of personality. The emblems that had dotted archive footage – posters, outfits, framed records, music video props – were gone. Bare walls and featureless rooms remained.

But then they came to the west wing, which had been converted into a giant, three-storey jungle gym. Netted walkways, trampolines, slides, padded bars and ball pits surrounded them. 'This could, of course, be stripped out,' Harriet noted. *The playthings maybe,* Andrea thought, *but not the residue of what happened here.* Seeing this room in all its physical glory brought those horror stories home; they ruptured through any of the marketing veneer. When she looked at the crown-shaped ball pit, she saw the scandalous photographs that had been published – naked children among the plastic balls, faces and genitals blurred. She heard the echoes of the survivors' tales, the 'games' DaSilva had made them play here during his sleepover parties. The walls were lined with funhouse mirrors, twisting all reflection to nightmarish distortion.

Being here in the room made her feel closer to those children, but like the vision in those mirrors, the truth was elusive. Just two months after the allegations first broke, the fightback to clear DaSilva's name began. His daughter released a documentary on YouTube featuring testimony from other kids who'd spent time at the Castle, and claimed to witness nothing unsavoury, alongside photo analysts who posited that the images may have been manipulated. Doubt sown, conspiracies bloomed. Sales of DaSilva's records actually spiked with all the media attention and there was talk of a new collection of previously unreleased recordings.

Since the opportunity to visit the Castle arrived, Andrea had decided to find the truth. She was tired of writing puff pieces about California's app bros. There could be a real, important story here. One that could change things. That could catapult her into *real* journalism, where her writing could have an impact on the world. So here she was with Xand Goetz, wandering why he – or anyone – would want to buy this place.

Xand had founded Vendor just five years ago, but had soared through the Silicon Valley ranks on the way to his first billion through the genius of his 'dynamic, integrated, fast and secure payment processor'. Which was a lot more lucrative than it sounded.

But the more time Andrea spent with him, the more she thought maybe he was just a man with money – too much money. The only story she wanted to cover was hidden in this fortress. Though it had been emptied over the past decade, there was a chance some secrets had gone undetected. During the past week, Andrea had managed to track down the source of the Dante photographs – a maid who used to work at the property. She'd spoken to the woman on the phone, a line weak with interference and failing memory, and found the tip. *The gold diamond...*

'This is the keep,' Harriet said. 'The heart of the Castle. Where the... former owner lived.' It was a block set into the back section of the building, with its own entrance from the courtyard. Harriet opened the doors, and they came into a marble lobby. In the centre was a statue. A life-size golden cast of Dante DaSilva.

'Holy shit,' Xand said.

'Yes, indeed,' Harriet replied. 'The owners haven't, ah, managed to get that removed as yet. It seems to have been bored into the foundations. The owners have been getting quotes to have it melted down in situ.'

Andrea approached the figure. It glinted in sunlight channelled through well-placed windows around the room. He was all there – the signature shades, braces, jacket, luxurious mane of hair. As she got closer, she saw the fine layer of dust gracing the gold. *Even a king needs someone to polish him*, she thought. She circled the statue. And almost gasped.

'Let me show you the master suite,' Harriet said. 'It is, truly, a sight to behold. If you follow me.' She indicated a glass elevator at the back of the lobby. Xand stepped towards it.

Andrea tensed. This could be her only chance.

'I, um… is there another way up?' she said. Xand frowned at her. 'I get horribly claustrophobic.'

Harriet softened. 'I'm afraid this is the only way, hon. It's perfectly safe though?'

'Sorry.' Andrea grimaced. 'I might have to sit this one out.'

Xand shrugged and stepped into the elevator with his assistant. Harriet pushed a button and they rose out of sight.

Andrea sprang into action. This had to be it. The back of the statue's jacket, a palm-sized gold diamond. It was raised. She ran her fingers around its edge, dug her nails in. 'Fuck!' she whispered as the cold metal prised at her nails. But there was give. This piece of the statue was separate. She tugged. It loosened. And with a clunk, it came away.

In its place was a diamond shaped hole, an entrance to the hollow figure, its edge rimmed with magnetic strips. She heard footsteps from the room above her, Harriet's muted laugh. Plunging a hand into the statue –

Empty. Breath ragged, palms sweating, she felt all round the crevasses. And there, tucked right in the bottom corner, was something. She pulled it out into the light, giving it a shake. It was a metal canister, the kind used to store a reel of film.

Above, more footsteps. Donk of shoes on the elevator floor. Whirring of its mechanism. Andrea thrust the canister into her bag. Just as the elevator descended, she managed to plant the diamond seal back into place.

'Are you alright?' Harriet asked.

Andrea brushed a stand of loose hair from her damp forehead. 'Yes. Just, a little anxious. The, er, the elevator.'

'Of course,' Harriet said.

As their car pulled away from the Castle, Andrea didn't look back. She felt a dawning realisation. Whatever footage this film contained, whatever story it gave her, whatever it proved... There was no guarantee it would change anything. People would still question the evidence, weaving whatever it showed into their theories. This story, like the singer at its heart, like the Castle in their rear-view, was too big for a simple, universal explanation.

'I think I'm gonna buy it,' Xand said, gazing out at the passing trees.

'Really?' Andrea said. Then, 'Why?'

'At the price it's dropped to, that place is a steal.' He smiled. 'I'll smarten it up a bit. Get it ready for entertaining clients, employee retreats, luxury vacation rentals. People will wanna come here for the thrill, whether they're fans or just morbidly curious. And if that doesn't work...' He shrugged. 'It's fourteen-hundred acres. That's always a solid investment.'

Andrea turned away, looking out her own window. Her bag felt heavy, and she held it close.

THE ONE WHO TOOK HER

The whole world knew him, and yet no one did. He was an abstract, a concept. Like love or complex numbers. In many ways, like God. But of course he wasn't. Paul Mackenzie was just a man. In many ways, ordinary. Except for what he knew. Except for what he *did*.

The whole world knew *her*, of course. They knew her name, her cherub face, glistening blonde hair and eyes all swollen with innocence. Her image was as familiar as the Mona Lisa. Her final portrait, snapped at the hotel pool, printed onto the heart and mind of the globe through years of repetition. Every newspaper, every television station, since the day she was taken.

Since the day Paul Mackenzie took her.

•

It wasn't the crime that made him special, it was the knowledge. Her final days were gospel. The story of the weeks, days and hours leading up to her disappearance poured over by journalists, amateur sleuths, professional sleuths and her mother's ghost writer, the real author of *My Victoria*. But each rendition ended the same: and then she was gone.

Of course, there were theories. She wandered off! She was sold to gypsies! Abducted by aliens! Killed by the parents!

But in a total void of hard evidence, no theory took hold. So one of the most famous stories on earth remained unfinished, a mystery. Only one knew the ending. Even two decades later, this thought filled Paul with awe.

In his childhood heart he believed he'd be special. The bitter irony of its realisation was that he alone could recognise he'd fulfilled that potential. To tell would be to ruin it.

Paul wasn't an evil man. No more than most that bound their way through life, knocked between opportunities and mistakes with little more control than the metal sphere in a pinball machine.

He thought about Vicky's family often. Hell, in the year after it happened, he thought he'd never escape their grief-ravaged faces, rasping desperation from every screen and front page he passed. They even stalked his dreams, his nightmares. *Come forward*, they said. *Come forward*.

Suffering made him sad. It always had, ever since he was a kid seeing animals kicked and pulled around by his buddies. He'd look away and cover his ears to blot out the squeals of pain. So he closed the paper, turned off the TV and said sorry to the blank screen. Paul wasn't a sadistic killer. No, he wasn't sadistic.

He even cared about the public who'd come to love her. They yearned to see her returned safe and sound, of course they did. But they yearned to know what happened more than anything. Over the years they'd come to accept that even the discovery of her body – however mutilated and decayed – would satisfy their need for closure. Paul could relate to this. He hated ambiguity, authors who died mid story, cancelled TV shows. He appreciated their need for an ending.

But he could never give it.

•

Why didn't he come forward? The question itched at the back of his mind day after day. Because he was scared. Because it wasn't that simple. Because he had everything to lose and nothing to gain. Because they would want to know *why*.

Why did he take her? The truth was Paul didn't really know. He wasn't a thief, or a child trafficker, a serial killer or a paedophile – he *thought* he wasn't a paedophile. The closest to truth he could boil the mess down to was unsatisfying: he saw her and he wanted her.

Paul wanted to have her. For her to be his.

Once a collector, always a collector. It was a craving as strong as the need for food and shelter. As a child, he'd built his own zoo of found animals. It started as bugs in boxes and ended when he caged the neighbours' cat in his back garden. His mum had found out and she had been *fuming*. They had moved soon after. She hadn't understood.

It was the same with the cat. He saw it across the street and just knew it was meant to be his.

He'd caught sight of the girl as he'd passed the café. She was glowing in magnificence, a whole spectrum brighter than the world around her. Paul had watched, agape.

But a child of thirteen was harder to take than a pet kitty. So he'd followed, observing as she and her family went about their Mediterranean holiday. He watched their games, their meals, and where they went home at night. He watched and he waited.

Paul could even now close his eyes and recall that morning in hyper detail. Relive the steps he took towards their hotel after he'd seen the parents leave without her. Feel the warm summer breeze ruffling the hair at the back of his neck. Hear the crickets in the trees.

Vicky's room was secluded, on the ground floor with its own French doors, and he walked up to it with no hesitation. He must do what he was here to do. Though he'd never broken in anywhere before in his life, he slid open her door as if second nature.

And there she was, waking in her bed, turning, looking… looking at him. She was feverish, he would later learn – the reason her parents had left her to rest while they sought out a pharmacy – but she smiled. He'd always remember that smile, it was in many ways the highlight of their time together. He beckoned. If she had not come, Paul would have retreated in acceptance. But she didn't. Because she knew what was meant to be. She came willingly into his outstretched arms. And he lifted her out, holding her close like a father.

He felt as much a father to her in that moment as he ever did with his real daughter, later.

Heart seemingly stilled along with his breath, Paul turned and carried her away, not bothering to close the doors. She was his now, and that was all that mattered. He carried her down the quiet streets, a pyjamared girl half-asleep, half-delirious, breathing softly with her arms clasped around his neck. To all the world she was his daughter. He even passed a couple of people and Paul was quietly amazed none moved to stop him. *Walk with authority*, he thought, *and none will question you.*

And none ever did.

•

Three hours later the screams began. And they pursued him across the years.

The screams of the parents, the public, the media. After only a couple of days, like with the neighbours' cat he once sought to possess, he knew he could not keep her.

He'd been transient for almost two years and drove on with her beside him, kept docile with cola and sleepy pills.

He could not sleep himself. The hunt was on. He felt it ringing at the back of his temples, a rising pitch that threatened to overwhelm him.

So Paul put her to sleep one final time and shed a tear as he laid her to rest where she would not be found.

•

In life, you had to be selfish. It was a hard lesson, but one Paul had accepted. You could deny it in public, but in your heart you knew it to be true.

He could never tell what he did, no matter the ease it might bring to many who existed in an eternal torment between hope and fear. Because she had saved him, renewed the soulless half-life he had been trudging through up to the day they met. Paul truly believed in every way, Vicky was sent for him.

He had sold the tainted car, returned to his homeland and started afresh. Buoyed with purpose, he carved out a new, restored existence for himself. He married and had a child.

Paul, the family man. Now that was something far too precious to destroy.

But Paul was not heartless. Never had been, never would be. He'd simply bounced through his own mistakes and opportunities of life. Coming out well the other side was a blessing, but an inevitable curse for the lives he'd hurt along the way.

He wept for them, every year. Every anniversary of that day. Every appeal. Every cry for resolution. And this year was a big one, twenty years since. His daughter was now the age *she* had been, would ever be.

His daughter's face turned from Vicky's immortal picture on the telly, up to her father's, a tear rolling down his cheek.

'Who is that?' she asked.

Paul told her.

'But what happened to her?' His daughter's face was full of innocent curiosity, uncorrupted by the darkness life brings.

After a moment, Paul answered. 'I took her.'

She stared at him for a moment, then burst into laughter. 'Don't be silly, Dad,' she said. 'Of course you didn't.'

Paul took her hand, and smiled.

MARCEL BELL SAVES THE WORLD

There's nothing so beautiful as the sunrise on Isla Primera, the reds and pinks glinting off the waves, bathing the shore, and illuminating the auburn strands of Wife Number Three's hair between your fingers as she noshes you off like her livelihood depends on it (it does). This is the life. It's a cliché, but my life really is *the* life. The pinnacle of pinnacles, such as has never been reached by any individual before in human history. In every respect, I have fucking nailed it.

Job done, Talia slides off onto the sand beside my lounger. As well she might. Here's what she said when she first flew into Primera: 'I don't like pebble beaches.' Well. Do you know how much it costs to ship an industrial crusher across the Atlantic to pulverise two kilometres of pebbled shoreline into dunes as silky as Arabian coke? Just shy of four mill. Two million dollars a fucking kilometre. She should be sleeping out on the beach at that price.

But today is not a day for grouching. Today is the day I change the world forever.

Of course, you could argue that I changed the world already with NervTech (and I'd accept that). But this is bigger. Far bigger.

Across the water, Isla Segunda floats on the horizon. The star of today's show is vast enough to overshadow anything else on the smaller island, jutting up proudly into the sky. Saviour V, the culmination of fifteen years of R&D. The dawn of a new enterprise. This rocket – *my* rocket – is going to pioneer a new industry, make me a fuck-ton money, and drop-kick the human race into the fucking galactic A league. Oh, and it's going to save the world too.

I got the global warming bug in the mid-noughties. NervTech had made me the fifth richest man on the planet, having virtually monopolised the gaming and processing market, and I was enjoying some time off. I'd taken my daughter on a sightseeing trip over the Antarctic ice sheets, soaring over the alien landscape in a helicopter custom designed to blast through the frozen skies. Seeing those icy cliffs collapsing into the ocean brought it home to me: the future, my legacy, that annoying Al Gore movie. This shit was *real*. And I thought: someone's got to start doing something about this.

As soon as our copter touched down on the yacht, I got my assistants on the phones, and we flew in the world's top eco boffins from across the globe for a crisis conference right there on the fucking deck.

'Right. How are we gonna fix this planetary problemo?' I asked them.

I won't bore you with the responses – most of it was wind turbine this, nanny state that – but one of the blokes caught my attention. He'd been investigating something called solar radiation management. 'When a super volcano erupts,' he explained, 'it shoots particles into the upper atmosphere. These can reflect the sun's rays and cool down the earth for up to two years. If we could find a way to do that mechanically, well, that could halt climate change.'

I hired him on the spot. Within two months he was heading up a crack team of eggheads in my new experimental venture, GeoTech. When others see visions of doom, I see business booming. That's how you succeed. You take on the challenges no one else wants to, and you take them on fast. I got where I am through forty-five years of graft. If you're not the hardest working person at your company, you shouldn't be running it. And I should know – I run five. On average I put in 36-hour shifts, seven days a week (accounting for my cognitive processing power, which is estimated to be 1.8 times that of the typical man).

A cough disturbs me. 'Marcel?'

'Yes?' I turn to see Jenny, one of my PAs. She glances down at me before looking away, blushing. Honestly, what's the point in owning a private island if you can't have your cock out? I sigh and cover myself with my robe. 'Spit it out.'

'We've had the final word from the regulators. We've been pushing them down to the wire – as you know – but they won't budge. It's a no.'

'Honey,' Talia says, gazing up from the sand with the wide-eyed naivety of a woman half her age (which would be thirteen – so a girl, I suppose), 'does that mean it won't be happening?'

'Course it doesn't,' I snap. 'Tell them to go ahead,' I say to Jenny.

'Marcel,' she says. 'It's a hard no. The DoD's got involved. They're threatening to shoot the rocket down if we proceed.'

'They won't.'

'There are five crew members in the module.'

'They won't,' I repeat.

I'm on the verge of mankind's greatest leap since that knucklehead hopped onto the moon, and I will not be held back by some bloody pen-pushers worried about 'unanticipated side effects'. My team has slaved for years to get this far. Rivers of blood and sweat have carried us here, with much of that fluid my own. Our technology is beyond cutting edge; it's cut *through* the edge. Saviour V will deposit its sulphate payload into the stratosphere, creating a fine organic sunshade that will be the first step in healing the Earth. If this is successful – which I'll make fucking sure it will be – before the decade is out, GeoTech will have monthly launches from hubs on every continent, dispersing our compound into an AI-driven mesh that will regulate the world's climate. You see, this isn't just about global warming. When we're done, I'll supply the fucking weather. Imagine it: every farm in America (of which I own 40% – it pays to invest in land) choosing its next rainfall from an app. Boosting agricultural productivity across Africa to lift millions out of poverty. Slapping a drought on Putin the next time he pisses someone off.

'Quick business lesson for you, Jenny. You don't get anywhere by asking for permission. You ask for forgiveness.'

And if this succeeds, they'll be falling over themselves to congratulate me, because – guess what – they'll want what I'm selling. It's funny really, how these governments can be so scared of our technological advances, while fawning at my feet. You want to know the trick? Give wisely.

That's right. I'm now the world's richest man, and I'm the world's most generous philanthropist. States would *literally* cease to function without my donations. So I'm invited to speak at every conference, advise on every policy, so they can beg for my investments. What's laughable is they're even too scared to acknowledge that the money I give them is but a fraction of the haul saved through our creative accounting. (If you want the secret: register your IP in Bermuda, then lease it out to your company and technically you never make a profit anywhere you'd have to pay taxes!) Charities adore me, NervTech fanboys toss themselves off to my every tweet and even the consumers that despise me can't help but use my products – *every single day*.

Besides, if the whole radiation management thing fails, I've got another brainbox working on Plan B – Operation Suckerpunch. We'll just blast a hole in the atmosphere and let all the nasty gasses out like a fart from under the duvet.

'Jenny, give the launch team the go ahead. My orders.'

'OK, Marcel,' she says quietly.

I sigh. 'Look, if it goes tits up, we'll drop a couple hundred mill into cancer tech. Or we'll open source the AIDS vax. All will be peachy, trust me.'

She nods, and makes the call.

Now comes the thunder from over the water. Gooseflesh ripples up my arms. Talia grips my ankle, but I shake her off. I rise, shrugging off my robe, and walk towards the sea. This is the birth of my new age, and I'll enjoy it naked if I want to.

Flames blossom on the horizon and Saviour V shudders into life. With an almighty boom, the rocket tears away from the earth, renting the sky in its wake. I close my eyes for a moment, arms wide, conducting my astral symphony. When I open them, I see another light, streaking across the sky. A white arrow, heading straight for my rocket.

'Shit. Shit shit shit,' Jenny is saying. 'They hit the button!'

Talia starts to scream.

Ah, fuck it.

'Jenny, better make that three hundred for the cancer.'

ABOUT THE AUTHOR

George T Riley is a writer and filmmaker based in Reading, Berkshire. You can explore more of his work through photography, films and stories on his website:

www.gtriley.com

Printed in Great Britain
by Amazon